THE HAUNTED CAVE

Don't miss any of the chilling adventures!

SPOOKSVILLE

THE HAUNTED CAVE

Christopher Pike

Aladdin

NEW YORK LONDON TORONTO SYDNEY NEW DELHI

ALADDIN
An imprint of Simon & Schuster Children's Publishing Division
1230 Avenue of the Americas, New York, NY 10020
This Aladdin edition October 2014
Copyright © 1995 by Christopher Pike
Cover illustration copyright © 2014 by Vivienne To
All rights reserved, including the right of reproduction
in whole or in part in any form.
ALADDIN is a trademark of Simon & Schuster, Inc.,
and related logo is a registered trademark of Simon & Schuster, Inc.
For information about special discounts for bulk purchases,
please contact Simon & Schuster Special Sales at 1-866-506-1949
or business@simonandschuster.com.
Cover designed by Jessica Handelman
Interior designed by Mike Rosamilia
The text of this book was set in Weiss Std.
Manufactured in the United States of America 0914 OFF
2 4 6 8 10 9 7 5 3 1
Library of Congress Control Number 2014946903
ISBN 978-1-4814-1055-7 (pbk)
ISBN 978-1-4814-1056-4 (hc)
ISBN 978-1-4814-1057-1 (eBook)

1

ADAM FREEMAN WAS HAVING ICE CREAM with his friends when the subject of the Haunted Cave came up. The ice-cream parlor was called the Frozen Cow, and it supposedly offered a choice of fifty flavors. They were listed on a large colorful bulletin board that hung behind the counter where the grumpy old man who owned the place stood. But the owner—even when asked politely—refused to give any customer anything but vanilla. Even chocolate and strawberry weren't available. Sally explained that the owner—whom she called Mr. Freeze—was a purist and believed that vanilla was the only ice cream worth serving. Adam had managed to persuade the man to make him a vanilla milkshake.

Of course, since this was Spooksville, Adam had to pay Mr. Freeze double not to use spoiled milk.

"Did you know that monkeys and apes love ice cream?" Watch said, working on a banana split that was made of bananas, vanilla ice cream, and nothing else. "Gorillas like it as well, although I've heard they'll only eat chocolate ice cream."

"They wouldn't like this place," Sally Wilcox muttered, frantically licking a melting ice-cream cone as if it would explode if she lost a drop.

"I thought monkeys and apes were vegetarians," Cindy Makey remarked.

Sally chuckled. "A vegetarian can eat ice cream. You don't kill the cow to get the milk out, you know. You just tug on the udders."

Cindy gave an exaggerated sigh. "I know that. I mean I thought that monkeys and apes *preferred* fruit to dairy products."

Watch shook his head. "That's not so. They're like kids—they'll take ice cream over bananas any day. And as far as I'm concerned, that proves Darwin's theory of natural selection. Man—and woman—evolved from monkeys. We're nothing but talking apes."

"But that's only a theory," Adam protested. "I don't believe it."

"You're reacting to the idea emotionally," Watch said. "It upsets you to think your ancestors used to need a shave twenty-four hours a day. In scientific matters you have to be cold and dispassionate."

"Look who's having the bananas," Sally muttered.

"I'm not reacting emotionally," Adam replied, insulted. "Science has never proven that we evolved from apes. You're forgetting the missing link."

"What about it?" Watch asked.

"It's still missing," Adam said, having a sip of his shake.

"What's the missing link?" Cindy asked.

"A non-vegetarian monkey," Sally said.

"It's a creature that would be half ape, half human," Watch explained. "Adam has a point. Science has never positively found a creature that is directly between us and apes on the evolutionary scale." Watch paused and glanced at Sally. "Of course not many scientists have been to Spooksville."

Sally shook her head vigorously. "Don't start talking about that. We're not going there, no way."

"Going where?" Adam wanted to know, certain he'd missed part of the conversation.

Watch leaned closer and lowered his voice. "The Haunted Cave."

Sally cringed. "Don't say it. To even speak the name will curse us."

"He already said it," Cindy said. "And there's no such thing as a curse."

Sally snorted. "Listen to the girl whose brother was kidnapped by a ghost last week. This whole town is cursed. I know, I was born here."

Cindy smiled. "Yeah, now that you mention it, I guess I can see the damage."

Adam chuckled. "Sally was cursed in the womb."

Sally fumed. "For your information I was born on Friday the thirteenth, which is practically a religious holiday in this town."

"So?" Adam said, puzzled.

"She's saying she wasn't cursed until she was born," Watch explained. "Anyway, this cave is fascinating. There are plenty of stories about creatures inside the cave that could be the missing link."

"Have you ever seen these creatures?" Adam asked skeptically.

"No, but I think a friend of mine did," Watch said. "His name was Bill Balley. He was a camera nut. He went in to photograph them and that was the last we heard of him."

"They found his camera though," Sally said. "It was smeared with blood."

"I think it was peanut butter and jelly," Watch said. "There was film in the camera. I helped develop it. The negatives were in lousy shape but one shot showed a blurry image of a hairy manlike creature."

"How big was the creature?" Adam asked.

"Hard to say," Watch said. "I couldn't tell how far away it had been taken, and there were no reference objects."

"It was big enough to eat Bill," Sally said.

"But I'd guess a missing link should be small," Adam said. "If it's half man, half ape."

"Bill probably thought the same thing," Sally retorted.

"I don't believe any of this," Cindy said.

Sally got mad. "You just moved here a month ago. You don't know anything about this town; therefore, your opinion is totally worthless."

Cindy turned to Adam. "Why don't we go have a look at this cave and prove to these guys there are no missing links running around this town?"

"I believe they run under the town," Watch said.

Adam considered. "We could do that, but I don't think we want to go inside the cave."

"Why not?" Cindy asked.

"Because one of these creatures might eat you alive," Sally said. "Adam knows that, but he's too much under your spell to say it out loud."

"I'm not under nobody's spell," Adam said angrily.

Sally snorted. "You're not under *anyone's* spell. You get so dizzy when you sit next to Cindy you can't even speak right."

"Why are you always yelling at Adam?" Cindy demanded.

"Because I believe he can be helped," Sally explained patiently. "Unlike some people I know."

Cindy stood. "Where is this cave? I want to go there right now. I want to see these creatures—*if* they really exist."

Watch checked one of his four watches. "It's getting late. You might want to explore the cave tomorrow."

"Bill disappeared later in the day," Sally added.

"It makes no difference what time of day we go in the cave," Cindy said. "As long as we have flashlights. Isn't that right, Adam?"

"Right," Adam agreed reluctantly. But even though he had lived in Spooksville for only two weeks, he had seen enough to know there might be something behind Watch's strange story. He didn't want Cindy thinking he was a coward, but he wished they could bring a hunting rifle as well as flashlights. Something powerful enough to stop a large hairy creature.

2

THE HAUNTED CAVE WAS LOCATED NEAR the town reservoir. Up in the hills behind Spooksville. The path to the cave was rugged, so they weren't able to take their bikes. As a result they didn't reach the cave until nearly seven. It was summer and the days were long, but the sun was already close to the horizon.

The opening of the cave didn't look scary. It was just a narrow crack in the rocky hillside that faced the reservoir. The entrance wasn't high—a grown man would have to stoop to get inside. Adam poked his head in and peered around with one of the flashlights they'd picked up at Watch's. All he saw were dirt walls, nothing spectacular.

"I don't see any creatures," he said as he pulled his head back out.

"That's what I call a thorough search," Sally said sarcastically. She pointed to the ground at Adam's feet. "That's where they found Bill's camera. I think they found some of his skin as well."

"That wasn't skin—it was his lunch bag," Watch said. He also peered in the cave, using the other flashlight they had brought. "It goes way back. In fact, I've heard it goes down deep and its tunnels wind around under most of the city."

"Is there another entrance?" Adam asked.

"Not that I know of," Watch said, straightening up.

Cindy appeared anxious to get going. "Well, are we going inside or what?"

Watch shook his head. "I think I'll wait out here for you guys."

"Why?" Adam asked. "You always like a good adventure."

"I think one of us should be here in case you don't come back," Watch said. "I can tell your families not to set places for you at dinner. Stuff like that."

"I can stay," Sally offered quickly. "I don't like caves much anyway."

"Coward," Cindy said.

Sally was instantly furious. "How dare you call me a coward? Why, when you were playing with Barbie and Ken, I was out fighting witches and warlocks."

Cindy was not impressed. "Then why are you afraid to explore the cave with Adam and me?"

Sally wore a mocking smile as she turned to Adam. "Is brave and resourceful Adam ready to explore the cave with dear, spunky Cindy?"

Adam hesitated. Standing near the entrance, he could feel a faint warm breeze coming from inside. He wondered where it came from. The air in most caves was cooler than the outside air. There was also a faint smell to this air. He was reminded of a barbecue, of the odor of dying coals.

"I think we could go in a little way and look around," Adam said finally.

"The creatures are supposed to live way in the back," Watch said. "You won't see anything if you just go in a few feet."

Cindy grabbed Watch's flashlight. "I say we go in all the way. But stay here if you want, Sally. We'll understand if you're too chicken. Adam and I don't need your help."

Sally smoldered. "I dislike being called chicken. Especially by a girl who couldn't rescue her own baby brother from a senile ghost."

Cindy held up a finger to Sally's face. "And who fought hand to hand with the ghost? It was Adam and me."

"And who figured out who the ghost really was?" Sally shot back.

"I did," Watch said.

"Really?" Adam asked. That was news to him.

"Listen," Sally interrupted. "I'm not afraid to explore this cave. I just don't want to get my hair dirty because I washed it this morning."

Cindy snorted. "You're just afraid of having your hair ripped out of your head."

"That is never pleasant," Watch said. "Sally, if you don't want to go inside, that's all right with me. We can sit here and shout words of encouragement if they start screaming."

"That's very noble of you," Adam said.

Sally stood, undecided. "If we do go in, and do see anything that might eat us—anything at all—we get out quick."

Adam nodded. "That sounds reasonable." He checked the flashlight he was carrying. They had picked them up at Watch's house. "Are the batteries fresh?"

"They should last a few hours," Watch said.

Adam nodded. "I'm sure we won't be gone that long."

He ducked inside the cave, Cindy and Sally following at his heels. Adam didn't know it at the time, but he was going to be in the cave much longer than any flashlight would last.

3

THE INTERIOR OF THE CAVE WAS DEFINITELY warmer. Adam noticed the change in temperature the moment he stepped in. The warmth continued to puzzle him. The air currents were definitely blowing out of the cave, not into it. He wondered if there wasn't another entrance nearby.

The size of the cave seemed to expand the moment they were inside. The ceiling was higher than his bedroom ceiling by at least two feet. The walls—six feet apart—were not the simple dirt he had imagined from the outside. Touching them, Adam saw that they were only coated with dust. Actually, the walls were made of hard black rock, which felt smooth beneath Adam's fingers.

Cindy studied the section of wall beside him. "It's like the volcanic rock in Hawaii," she said, carrying the other flashlight.

"You've been to Hawaii?" Sally asked with a huff. "Must be nice."

"We used to go regularly before my father died," Cindy said quietly.

"Are there any geysers around Spooksville?" Adam asked Sally.

"Besides your temper," Cindy added.

"The fountain at the city hall explodes in steam every now and then," Sally said, throwing Cindy a nasty look. "No one knows why."

Adam gestured with his light to a tunnel that ran deeper into the cave. It definitely sloped down, in the direction of the city. "Do you guys notice that faint burning smell?" he asked. "I think there might be hot lava down there."

"That's one good reason to turn back now," Sally muttered.

"I don't know," Cindy said. "The smell and the heat might just be from a hot spring. I want to go deeper."

"Why are you so excited to meet an ape man?" Sally asked.

Cindy shrugged. "If there really are such creatures in here, it would be the discovery of a lifetime."

"If there really are such creatures in here," Sally countered, "your lifetime might be very short."

They moved farther down into the cave. The tunnel became steep, and they had to crouch down to keep from slipping. Soon they were practically on their butts, and their pants were getting dirty. Adam worried that if it got any steeper they'd need a rope to climb out. He was about to suggest they turn back when they heard a faint sound coming from deeper inside the cave. It echoed for several seconds, like an otherworldly lullaby, haunting and hypnotic. It didn't sound like a monster, but it didn't sound human either. The three of them froze.

"What was that?" Cindy whispered.

"It doesn't sound like Bill," Sally whispered back.

"Shh." Adam held up his hand. The sound did not repeat itself, but it sure had their hearts pounding. Adam wiped sweat from his forehead. He had to strain to keep his voice calm. "I think there's something alive down there."

"Like we haven't been saying that all along," Sally said, hissing.

Adam glanced at Cindy, who appeared to be having second thoughts about making important scientific discoveries. "We could come back another time," he suggested. "When we have more time."

"When we're feeling suicidal," Sally added.

Cindy hesitated. "Did we really hear something? Or did we just imagine it?"

"You don't need an imagination in this town," Sally said. "Reality is nightmarish enough. I say let's get out of here before it eats us."

"I honestly do think there's something down there," Adam said to Cindy. He added, "And it doesn't sound like it's in a good mood."

Cindy thought for a moment more, then shrugged. "We can always come back later."

"That's my brave girl," Sally said.

They turned and started back up the slippery floor of the cave. Pushing and pulling on each other, they were able to make it back up to where the floor was relatively flat. By then they were sweating heavily and were anxious to get outside and draw in deep breaths of fresh air.

Adam could see the cave opening thirty feet in front of him. He could even see Watch through the entrance crack—no doubt watching the sun set. Adam was about to call out to him when the girls started fighting again for what seemed the millionth time.

"I never said it sounded like a scary creature," Cindy said. "I would have gone on."

"She says that now that she's running away," Sally said.

"Listen," Cindy snapped. "If anyone's running, it's you. We had to drag you in here in the first place."

Sally stopped and turned on Cindy. "I admit that I don't enjoy being in this cave. You'd have to be a caveman with a low caveman IQ to like it. But you—Ms. Archaeological Overachiever Herself—are bugging the heck out of me pretending to be brave. You're more scared than the rest of us. You're a hypocrite, in other words, and I can't stand hypocrites. They remind me of myself before I overcame my major psychological hangups." She added, "I don't see what Adam sees in you."

"Oh, brother," Adam said.

Cindy got up on her toes. "I bug you? You know that's like a rattlesnake saying to a well-mannered rabbit that the rabbit is annoying it. Just when the snake is about to bite the rabbit."

"I don't have a rattle," Sally snapped.

"Yeah, but you've got a poison tongue," Cindy said. "I wish for just once you would shut up. That you would close your mouth, shut it tight, and forget English and any other language you know for a twenty-four-hour period. Then maybe the rest of us—"

"Stop!" Adam shouted suddenly. He paused to stare

at the opening of the cave. The light from the outside had just flickered slightly.

"What is it?" Sally asked quickly.

Adam pointed to the opening. "Did any of you notice something move over there?"

"No," Cindy said.

"What do you mean?" Sally asked.

Adam frowned. "The entrance looks narrower."

"That's ridiculous," Sally said. Then she froze. "It is narrower!"

Cindy jumped in place. "The opening is closing! Let's get out of here!"

Cindy was right, the entrance was actually closing up. The smooth black rock could have turned molten. It seemed to flow together as they ran toward Watch and the outside. Watch had also noticed the change in the entrance size. But he wasn't foolish enough—or brave enough—to jump inside and try to rescue them. He waved to them, however, to hurry. Unfortunately, the second they reached the entrance, the edges pushed in closer, and the space looked too tight to squeeze through. Adam and Cindy and Sally looked at one another desperately. They were each thinking the same thing. If they tried to squeeze through and got stuck, would they be crushed to death?

"What should we do?" Cindy asked anxiously.

"We have to get out," Sally said. "Go first, Cindy. You're the skinniest."

"You're as skinny as me," Cindy said.

"But I have big bones," Sally said.

"Shut up!" Adam snapped, dropping to his knees beside the shrinking hole. He tried pulling the closing edges apart with his hands. Contrary to what he had thought, the material had not turned molten. The rock was still hard as, well, rock. But it wasn't behaving like ordinary rock. It was like the tree that had tried to eat him his first day in Spooksville. It seemed to be alive. Adam pulled his hands back inside, afraid they would be crushed. He shouted out to Watch, who was peering in at them.

"Go find a stick!" Adam yelled. "Maybe we can prop it open!"

"Gotcha," Watch said and disappeared. He came back a few seconds later; by then the entrance was a foot wide. He had a short stubby stick and a couple of medium-size rocks. He tried using the stick as a brace, but the closing edges snapped it in two as if it were a twig. The girls screamed.

"Put in the rocks!" Adam cried desperately. "We can't let it seal us inside!"

"I don't know what's causing this!" Watch said, straining to fit the rocks in the shrinking gap. "Bill never said anything about the cave entrance closing."

"Bill is dead!" Sally yelled. "Just stop it from closing!"

Watch managed to get one rock in place. But the closing of the cave seemed unstoppable. For one second the stone balanced tensely between the sides of the opening. Then a crack appeared in the center of the rock, and suddenly it burst into dust. Adam had to wipe the debris from his eyes. He could hardly see as Watch shouted at him.

"I don't know how to stop it!" Watch said.

"Do you know why it started?" Adam shouted back.

Watch was barely visible. "No!"

"Go for help!" Adam cried just before his friend vanished.

"Where?"

"Go——" Adam began. But he was too late.

He was talking to a smooth black wall.

The cave entrance was closed.

They were trapped inside. In the dark.

4

THEY HAD TWO FLASHLIGHTS, SO IT WASN'T
completely dark. The white beams reflected up over
their grim features. But inside, where they really lived,
all light had been extinguished. The cave had locked
them in. And they had no reason to believe it would ever
let them go. They sat in silence for several minutes by
the vanished entrance, hardly peeking at one another.
Finally Adam stirred. He was the boy, he told himself.
He was responsible for keeping them from despairing.

"There might be another way out," he said.

"There isn't," Sally mumbled, staring at the ground.

"You don't know that for sure," Adam said. "We have
to look."

"I don't want to look," Sally said. She gestured over her shoulder. "We might get eaten."

"Well, we can't sit here and do nothing." Adam was also staring at the ground. "Maybe we can dig our way out."

Sally felt the hard floor. "We'd need dynamite. Did you bring any?"

Adam felt the solid rock as well. It would take heavy equipment to drill through it. "No," he said quietly. "I forgot to bring any."

"I don't understand how this could have happened," Cindy whispered, her face pale.

"This is Spooksville," Sally said. "There's no understanding anything that happens here. The best you can do is not look for trouble." She added in a louder voice, "Like some of us wanted to do."

"You were the one who—" Cindy began.

"Let's not fight," Adam interrupted. "We don't have time." He tapped the side of his flashlight. "There isn't much energy in our batteries. If we don't find a way out before the lights give out, we'll never get out of here."

Sally sat up and stared hard at both of them. "I would like to hold one of the flashlights please."

"You can't have mine," Cindy said quickly.

"We'll stay together," Adam said. "It doesn't matter who carries the lights."

"Fine," Sally said. "Give me your light then."

"No," Adam said.

"Why not?" Sally asked. "I can hold it as well as you can. Give it to me."

"Why do you want it?" Cindy snapped.

"Because I'm afraid of the dark, bright brain," Sally said. Every kid who grew up in this town is. What do you need a light for? To fix your makeup?"

Adam held out his light. "Here. Take mine then, but turn it off. We'll use one light at a time to save batteries."

"I'll turn my light off first," Cindy said, catching Sally's eye. She nodded at her nemesis. "Because you're scared."

Sally nodded. "You'd better be scared, too."

Far below them, but maybe not so far away, they heard a faint noise again. Only this time it definitely sounded like a growl. The preying noise of some huge hungry creature. It echoed in their ears for ages before fading into a silence thicker than the blood that seemed to have turned to molasses in their hearts. Finally Adam swallowed and nodded in the direction of the sound.

"We have to go down that way," he said. "It's the only way out."

They started down, on their hands and knees this time. They were terrified of slipping. If they did, they might drop the flashlights. The bulbs might break, and then they wouldn't know what was in front of them, or what was coming at them from behind.

They reached the spot where they had turned back before, and it took a lot of courage to cross that line. Once over it they truly knew they couldn't go back. They moved as a single unit, practically holding on to each other.

"I wonder what Watch is doing," Cindy mumbled.

"He's walking home," Sally said. "Trying to figure out what to tell our parents."

"He could be going for help," Cindy said. "We could be rescued. Adam, maybe we should stay near the entrance."

Sally shook her head. "The authorities don't look for or rescue people in Spooksville. There are too many disappearances. They consider it a waste of time. Plus we lost half our police force in the last year."

"What happened to them?" Cindy asked.

Sally shrugged. "No one knows."

"Watch might be going to someone else for help," Adam said.

"Who would he ask?" Sally demanded, squeezing her light tight.

"Bum for one," Adam said. Then he added, "He might even go see Ann Templeton."

Sally sneered. "I'd rather face the creature down here than hope that evil witch would rescue us."

The creature might have heard Sally because it growled again. It definitely sounded hungry, maybe even excited. Perhaps it was coming their way, hoping to greet and eat them. The three of them stared at one another and Sally barely shook her head. She was taking back what she had just said, but it might have been too late for that.

5

ADAM KNEW HIS FRIEND WATCH WELL. WATCH
did indeed go for help, and Bum was at the top of his
list. Watch had a pretty good idea where Bum would
be. It was Friday evening, and everyone knew it was
Bum's custom to go to the only theater in town and try
to sneak in to catch one of the new releases. But since
the owner of the theater knew of Bum's habit, too, Bum
was rarely successful at getting inside. Watch caught
up with Bum just as he was being thrown out on the
sidewalk.

"What's playing tonight?" Watch asked, helping his
old friend up. Bum was dressed in his usual dirty gray
coat and smelled as if he hadn't taken a bath in two

weeks. But his bright green eyes had lost none of their humor. He laughed as he got to his feet.

"A horror film, as usual," Bum said. "It's a remake of *It: The Terror from Beyond*. The original was awful, so I don't mind missing the sequel." He paused and squinted at him. "How are you, Watch? You look worried."

Watch nodded. "I am. I took my friends up to the Haunted Cave and the entrance closed up on them. They're trapped inside."

Bum was amazed. "Why did you take them there?"

"Cindy Makey, the new girl in town, wanted to go."

"The one with the ghost for a granny?"

"Yeah, her. We saved her brother, but I don't know how we're going to save her now. Adam and Sally are with Cindy." Watch paused. It was never good to pressure Bum because he could clam up and tell you nothing. But Watch felt in a big hurry, which was unusual for him. "Do you know how to get the entrance to open up again?"

"Sure. You wait. It opens up again, eventually."

"How long does it take?"

Bum scratched his thinning hair. "Years."

"But they'll be dead by then."

"That is a problem." Bum leaned closer and spoke quietly. "Did you warn them about the Hyeets?"

"What's that?"

"The Bigfoots that live in the cave. They're a nasty lot. You know what happened to Bill Balley. The blasted creatures ate him alive. Ruined his final photo shoot."

Watch was concerned. "I didn't know they were called Hyeets, but I did warn the others about them."

Bum shrugged and looked down the block in the direction of the diner. "It doesn't matter if you warned them or not. The Hyeets will get them. Your friends are as good as dead. No sense worrying about them. Hey, how would you like to buy me dinner?"

Watch thought for a moment. "If I do, will you tell me everything you know about the Haunted Cave? And the Hyeets?"

"Deal." Bum grinned and slapped Watch on the back. "And if you get me dessert, I just might remember another way to get into the cave. You have money on you?"

Watch nodded and checked his watch set on West Coast time. The walk back to find Bum had been long and hard in the dark so his friends had been trapped for over an hour now. He wondered if he had put fresh batteries in the flashlights. Maybe he'd used old ones. He just hoped Bum could help in some way. At the moment Watch couldn't think of any other leads to pursue.

"I have money," Watch said almost to himself as they walked in the direction of the diner.

6

THE FLOOR HAD LEVELED OUT. THEY NO longer had to move forward on their hands and knees. The tunnel had also widened out so they weren't bumping into one another. These things were positive. Unfortunately the temperature had increased another ten degrees. They were sweating heavily and feeling terribly thirsty. Also, the flashlight Sally was carrying was beginning to dim. She shook it as they walked, trying to brighten the beam. They had been in the cave for two hours.

"This thing isn't going to last," Sally said.

Adam, walking on Sally's right, nodded. Cindy was on her left. "Let's just hope the second one has stronger batteries," he answered.

"It doesn't matter if it does if we don't know where we're going," Cindy said.

"You're a cheery character," Sally muttered.

"The queen of despair speaks," Cindy shot back.

"I would be at home watching TV and stuffing my face if you hadn't been so adamant about seeing this cave," Sally said.

"Just think of all the extra calories you're burning," Cindy replied.

"Would you two stop!" Adam said.

"Why should we stop?" Sally asked. "We're not low on oxygen. We might as well yell at each other in a desperate attempt to ward off the creeping horror that threatens to engulf our very souls."

"Well, if it makes you feel better," Adam said. But then his eyes took in a disturbing image. He stopped and pointed fifty feet up ahead. "What's that sticking out of the wall?" he asked, knowing the answer.

That was the arm of a skeleton. They approached it cautiously, with the light bobbing from Sally's trembling hand all the while. It was the last thing any of them wanted to find. The idea of being trapped inside the cave and eventually turning into skeletons was never far from their thoughts.

Yet this corpse didn't appear to have been trapped in

the cave, like them. "How could he have gotten in the wall?" Adam asked. Sally, of course, had her own theories.

"One of the ape creatures got him," she said. "Chewed him down to the bone, and stuffed him in there. It's obvious. It's probably what's going to happen to us."

"I don't know," Adam said. He nodded to Sally. "Give me the light."

"No," Sally said.

"I just want to look up ahead," Adam said.

"No," Sally said, hugging the flashlight close to her body.

"You can borrow Cindy's light until I come back," Adam said.

"She can't have mine," Cindy said quickly.

Adam frowned. "Then may I borrow your light?"

"Of course." Cindy handed it over. "What are you searching for?"

"Give me a minute and you'll see," Adam replied, flipping on the light. The glare from the second flashlight reminded them just how dim the first one was. Sally wanted to switch, but Adam wasn't in a negotiating mood. After telling the others to wait where they were, he moved carefully forward. Sally called after him.

"If something grabs you," she said, "scream real loud so we'll know to run the other way."

"Thanks," he muttered.

Two minutes and two hundred feet later, Adam found what he was looking for. It was a second skeleton, hanging partway out of the wall. Only this skeleton had portions of a rotting wooden box around him. Adam hurried back and collected the others, and then he showed them what he'd found. The girls were puzzled, and not too happy to see what they thought was a second victim of the ape creatures. But Adam shook his head.

"Don't you see?" he said. "This guy—if it was a guy— was buried in a coffin. The other corpse probably was as well, but his box just wore out over time."

Sally understood. "You're saying we're under the cemetery?"

"Exactly," Adam said.

"You act like that's good news," Sally said. "I mean, I can think of a lot better places to be."

"It's good that we know where we are," Adam explained.

"Why?" Sally asked.

"Maybe now we can plan which way to go," Adam said.

Sally gestured straight ahead of them. "It's only going one way, Adam. Straight to the monsters' kitchen."

"We'll see." Adam flicked off his flashlight. He was

shocked at how dark it was with only the first one on. They could hardly see one another. Yet the gloom gave him an idea. He reached out and yanked a board from the coffin out of the wall. The skeleton's skull bobbed up and down but the corpse didn't complain.

"What are you doing?" Sally asked. "That's the only home that guy's got, you know."

Adam continued to tug on the boards. "I want to take as many of these with us as we can. We have to prepare for both our lights running out. We might be able to use the wood as torches."

"That's a great idea," Cindy said, moving to help Adam.

"How are we going to light these torches?" Sally asked. "You're no Boy Scout, and Cindy and I are certainly not Girl Scouts. I couldn't kindle a spark into a campfire if you gave me a gallon of gasoline."

"Let's worry about that when we need to," Adam said.

Sally sighed, although she did begin to pull boards from the coffin. "This is great," she said. "When the ape creature goes to eat us, we can offer to build him a small house if he'll spare our lives."

Soon each of them had a small bundle of wood to carry. They started forward once more. They hadn't heard the creature growling in a while, and didn't know if that was a good sign or a bad one. In a way, Adam preferred it when the monster was making noise. At least then they knew where it was. There could be nothing worse than its sneaking up on them.

Five minutes after leaving the second skeleton, they came to a fork in the tunnel. They could go left or right. It was a difficult decision to make because both ways were dark and dangerous. Adam tried sniffing the air in each cave, searching for changes in temperature as well as foul odors. The cave on the right seemed to be cooler, but the one on the left was fresher smelling. He told the others what he had found. Of course the two girls immediately disagreed on which way to go.

"I want to go to the right," Cindy said. "We don't want to run into a lava pit."

"I think we should go to the left," Sally said. "The bad smell may be from things the ape creatures didn't completely eat."

"The right way doesn't actually smell bad," Cindy said, sniffing. "Its air is just stale."

"Dead things smell stale," Sally said.

"If we have just left the cemetery behind," Adam said, trying to get his directions straight, "then if we go right we should be right under the witch's castle."

"Then that settles it." Sally gasped. "We don't want to go anywhere near that place."

"But the castle has been there for ages," Adam said. "It might have a secret passage that leads down to this cave. We could use it to get out."

"And end up where?" Sally complained. "In the witch's living room. She'll roast us in her fireplace."

"You're thinking of the witch who looked like her on the other side of the Secret Path," Adam said. "Ann Templeton doesn't seem all that bad."

Sally shook her head. "I can't believe you. Ann Templeton smiled at you and told you you had beautiful eyes and you want to disregard all the evil things she's done to the kids in this town."

"I think you've made up half those things," Adam said.

"Maybe I have," Sally said. "But if the other half is true, you still don't want to get near her."

"I want to try my luck with the castle," Cindy said firmly. "I'm tired and thirsty. I don't know how much longer I can keep going like this."

"I'm not going that way," Sally said just as firmly.

"You have to," Adam said. "Your light is about to run out."

Sally sounded hurt. "You would leave me here alone in the dark to die? Just because Cindy wants to go right and

I want to go left? Adam, I thought you were my friend."

"I'm not leaving you to die," Adam said patiently. "We have to go one way or the other. If this way doesn't work out, we can come back and try your way."

Sally sighed again. "I have a bad feeling about this."

"You have bad feelings twenty-four hours a day," Cindy muttered.

"If you had grown up in this town you would understand," Sally replied.

7

THE SPACE NARROWED AS THEY TURNED TO
the right, and the temperature definitely fell. In fact,
it began to feel very cool. Adam took that as a good
sign. He stopped feeling so thirsty. But the clock was
still ticking. They couldn't wander around forever. Their
first flashlight was all but dead. To keep from bumping
into one another, they had to turn on the second. Adam
told Sally to save what little was left of the batteries in
the first. She turned it off and put it in her back pocket.

Ten minutes after leaving the fork, they came to a
huge open area. For a second Adam was ready to celebrate. He thought they had gotten out of the cave alto-
gether. But after setting down his sticks and searching

around with the beam of Cindy's light, he realized they weren't home yet. It was as if a large mine shaft had been sunk into the ground, and they had stumbled into the bottom of it. Circular walls surrounded them. But his light was not strong enough to reveal what was at the top of the shaft and how high up it went.

Adam saw that the cave did not continue on the other side.

There was only one way in, one way out.

"Where are we?" Cindy whispered.

"We may be under the castle," Adam said. "Do you think I should call out?"

"No," Sally said.

"Yes," Cindy said.

"Do what Cindy says," Sally whined. "You always do."

"That's not fair," Cindy snapped. "Adam's his own person. He makes his own decisions."

"Shh." Adam held up his hand. "I think I hear something."

What he heard was the faint clanging of metal. It seemed to be coming from directly overhead and on opposite sides of the shaft—two sources. Adam was reminded of the black knight on the other side of the Secret Path, the servant of the evil redheaded witch. The knight had creaked like an unoiled hinge as he walked. The people—or creatures—above them now did as well.

Faint orange lights began to glow a hundred feet above them on both sides of the shaft. Clearly there were two people approaching the shaft from opposite tunnels. But the sound of their heavy armor—for that was what it sounded like to him—worried Adam. He was on the verge of telling the girls to back out of the shaft when the flames of two torches seemingly burst out from the walls of the shaft. In reality, there was a narrow stone walkway far above them that the two creatures had stepped onto.

And they were definitely creatures, not humans.

They were man-size trolls. Their faces were squished and ugly. They looked as if their mothers had been lizards married to pigs. They had fat flat noses and angry red eyes that smoked with anger. They wore smooth steel breastplates, and in their right hands they carried broad silver swords. With their left hands, they held up their flaming torches. They gloated when they saw what had stumbled into their pit.

That was how Adam felt. As if they had stumbled into a trap.

He shouted at the girls. "Run back to the cave!"

They dashed for the opening, but before they could reach it a gate of metal bars fell down over the opening.

It smashed into the dirt floor, piercing the ground with long spikes. They all three tugged on it as hard as they could, but it refused to budge. Overhead Adam saw one of the trolls set his sword and torch down and reach for a long black spear. There was a chain attached to the base. Even before the troll attacked, it was clear what he and his partner intended to do. To spear the foolish human kids and haul them up to have for dinner. The creatures wanted their meat. Alive or dead.

The troll raised the spear over his head.

"Duck!" Adam cried to the girls.

The three of them hit the floor.

The spear struck the metal gate with a loud clang.

Sparks flew. They all cried out.

The troll had missed. But he didn't mind.

He would have all the chances he needed to catch them.

The troll pulled the spear back up by yanking on the chain attached to the base of it.

Adam leaped up. "Spread out," he called. "Keep moving. Make yourself a difficult target."

The shaft was maybe a hundred feet across. That was wide, but with two trolls standing above, Adam felt as if they were trapped in a narrow crevasse. The overhead walkway clearly circled the entire shaft. The troll with the torch helped his partner. While the one with the spear aimed, the other held the light out for him to get a clear view of his victim. Adam saw that they were aiming for him.

The troll threw his spear once more.

Adam jumped to the right.

The spear went through the space between his left arm and his left side. It tore his shirt; it had missed him by inches. The trolls laughed and their slobber dripped down into the shaft. They were enjoying the sport. Adam was so scared he couldn't move. Not even as the troll pulled the spear back up to where he was standing. The two trolls shifted position. They were going after Cindy next.

"Keep moving!" Adam shouted again, remembering to find his own feet.

But Cindy did the worst of all things. Staring up at the troll with the spear, terror in her eyes, she backed up against the stone wall. Standing almost still, she made a perfect target. Overhead, the troll raised his spear once more. Adam knew what was about to happen, but was too far away to stop it.

"Cindy!" he screamed. "Duck!"

She didn't. The spear flew through the dark air, headed right for her heart. Adam wanted to close his eyes. He couldn't bear to see her die.

But then, suddenly, Cindy went flying off to one side. Sally had tackled her.

The spear hit the rock wall and fell harmlessly to the ground.

Adam pumped his fist. "Yeah! Way to go Sally!"

Sally and Cindy jumped back up in an instant.

"You save me next time," Sally muttered, keeping her eyes on the trolls.

"Deal," Cindy said, gasping.

Adam ran over to them. "I have an idea," he said quietly. "But to make it work we have to gather back by the metal gate."

"They'll get one of us for sure if we do that," Sally protested.

"They'll get us all if we don't do something drastic," Adam said. "Trust me on this."

They hurried to the entrance. Already the troll had his spear back in hand. He laughed when he saw them standing so close together, standing so still. He drew back his arm.

"Jump to the side just as he lets go," Adam whispered, standing between the two girls.

"Which way are you jumping?" Sally asked on his right.

"You'll see," Adam said, reaching behind him and grabbing two bars of the metal gate.

The troll let his spear go.

It flew toward Adam.

Adam had known the troll would aim for him, since he was in the middle. He also thought the troll would aim low, figuring the stupid human boy would try ducking again. For that reason, Adam pulled himself up on the bars just as the spear flew toward him. He almost didn't pull himself up in time. The blade on the spear scratched his left leg as it stabbed past, drawing blood beside his knee. But Adam didn't mind because the spear landed exactly where he wanted it to. On the other side of the gate. As the troll growled and started to pull the spear back up, Adam jumped down and grabbed the spear.

Now Adam knew he was no match—strength-wise— for a troll. If he had a tug-of-war with the creature for the spear, he'd lose. Adam had something more clever up his sleeve. Before the troll could react, Adam pulled the tip of the spear out of the dirt, passed it and the chain it was attached to around one of the metal bars, and jammed it back into the ground.

Overhead the troll yanked hard.

But the spear stayed where Adam had jammed it.

The girls jumped to Adam's side and patted him on the back.

"Absolutely brilliant," Sally said.

"You're hero material," Cindy agreed.

"Let's not celebrate yet," Adam said quietly. "We can't push this gate up by ourselves, but maybe we can get the trolls to lift it for us. We have to get them real mad so they're not thinking. I just want them anxious to get their spear back."

"How do you get a troll mad?" Cindy asked.

"Just watch me," Sally said, turning to face their tormentors. She spoke in a loud, mocking voice. For once Adam was glad to hear it. "Oh, Mr. Trolls! It doesn't look like you'll be having dinner tonight. That's too bad. I feel real sorry for you guys. I know it must be a drag having to work down here in this dark dungeon. You're always on the night shift. I bet you guys never get out and see the sun. I can tell that just by looking at you. I mean, really, you guys are ugly. You're disgustingly gross. You look like frogs that swallowed too many hormones. Lizards that sucked up too much slime. I bet you guys can't even get a date with a girl troll. That hair sticking out of your noses is disgusting. You both need to see a barber. And didn't your mothers teach you any manners when you were baby trolls? You're not supposed to slobber over your food until you've killed it and drawn it out of the pit. It's lousy etiquette, plain and simple. A goblin would never behave that way."

Sally's antics had the desired effect. Even though they didn't understand exactly what she said, the trolls were instantly furious. They growled bitterly and their slobber dripped all over the place. They circled the overhead walkway until they were standing directly above the metal gate. Of course that was exactly what Adam was hoping for. Because as the trolls yanked hard on the chain, the chain slowly began to lift the gate upward. A crack appeared beneath the barrier, then a foot of space—two feet. That was enough for Adam.

"Get under it!" he shouted. Letting the girls go first, Adam grabbed several of the boards from the coffin and slid under the gate just behind Cindy. Above him he could hear the trolls screaming in anger. They released their hold on the chain, and the gate clanged down once more. But by then Adam and his friends were free, racing away at high speed and gasping with relief.

"I told you we should go to the left," Sally said, panting.

"You can say I told you so as many times as you want," Cindy said.

"As long as the other way doesn't turn out to be worse," Adam agreed.

8

WATCH HAD FED BUM A TURKEY DINNER
complete with mashed potatoes, gravy, and stuffing and
still he hadn't learned anything that could help free his
friends from the Haunted Cave. Bum was simply too
interested in his food to be worried about such trivial
matters as three trapped kids. The way Bum shoveled
down his white meat and buttered biscuits, Watch sus-
pected he hadn't eaten a decent meal in a week.

"Would you like anything else?" Watch asked, growing impatient. He hadn't ordered food for himself, only
a glass of milk, which tasted flat and chalky, like something out of Mr. Spiney's refrigerator. Mr. Spiney, the
town librarian, always added calcium to the milk he

made everyone drink so that it would make one's bones stronger. Mr. Spiney had a thing about strong bones, although he had lousy posture himself.

Bum nodded with a mouthful of food. "I'll have apple pie and ice cream as soon as I finish with this." He paused to look at Watch. "Are you sure you're not hungry?"

Watch lowered his head. "I'm not feeling hungry at all."

Bum nodded. "You're worried about your friends, I understand. Maybe I was a little hasty when I said to forget about trying to rescue them." He picked up his glass of water. Even though he was Spooksville's town bum, he never actually drank alcohol. He took a sip of his water and continued. "Maybe there's another way into the cave."

"You mentioned that earlier," Watch said, sitting up straight. "Do you know another way?"

Bum burped and picked at his potatoes. "No."

Watch fell back in his seat. "Oh."

"But because I don't know of one doesn't mean it doesn't exist." Bum paused. "Ann Templeton might know another way in."

"The town witch?"

"Yeah. She's a clever gal."

Watch removed his thick glasses and cleaned them on

his shirt. They often steamed up. "Did she really put a curse on you so you went from being town mayor to town bum?"

Bum chuckled. "If she did curse me, I was happy for it. Being a bum is much more fun than being mayor. You never have to attend any meetings. I used to hate all those meetings. People would sit around a table and talk about things none of them had the slightest interest in. It made me want to set city hall on fire."

"I thought you did set city hall on fire."

Bum scratched his chin. "Oh, yeah, that's right. That was the night the fire chief's wife was having her baby. City hall was always so ugly. I think the ash did more for it than a fresh coat of paint would have."

Watch put his glasses back on. Without them, he was legally blind. He hadn't been able to see well since his family had broken up and spread to all parts of the country. But that wasn't something he talked about with others. Even Sally did not know what he had gone through growing up in Spooksville. Watch had not had an easy childhood.

"Did you ever annoy Ann Templeton?" Watch asked. "If we're going to ask her for a favor, I'd like to know ahead of time."

Bum ran his hand through his stringy hair. "Well, I once proposed to the city council that we pave over the local cemetery and build a rec center on top of it. Since the cemetery is practically in her backyard, that might have made her mad. She did send me a skull in the mail the day after I made the proposal. I used it as a paper-weight for a month or two, until I was replaced,"

"Why did you want to put a rec center on top of a cemetery?" Watch asked.

Bum burst out laughing and slapped his knee. "I thought we could have wonderful Halloween parties with all those dead people beneath us!"

Watch had to smile. "The place does have a nice view. But back to talking to Ann Templeton. Do you know where she is right now?"

Bum glanced at one of Watch's watches. The service at the diner was awful. It had taken forever to get Bum's food. Over three hours had passed since Watch last saw his friends. It was close to eleven.

"At twelve she'll go to the grocery store," Bum said. "She always buys her food on Friday at midnight. She doesn't trust any of her servants to do the shopping. She doesn't have many human ones anyway. The store stays open just for her in fact. They're afraid to close until she's done with her business. Once they did shut early on a Friday, and the next day the meat cutter was found frozen to death in the meat locker."

"Did he have a meat hook through his brain?" Watch asked.

"No. He had choked to death on an ice-cream bar. Whether it was her fault, I don't know. But they always treat her real nice at the market."

"Earlier you called the ape creatures in the cave Hyeets," Watch said. "Where does that name come from?"

"That's what the Native Americans who used to live around here called the creatures," Bum explained. "They really are the Bigfoots the TV programs sometimes do special reports on. They're the missing link—the bridge between humans and apes. You have to respect them. They get more press than most of our local politicians."

"Are they intelligent?" Watch asked.

Bum was thoughtful. "I don't know. They're always hungry, that's for sure. But since they live underground where there's not much food, they can't be too smart."

Watch hesitated. "Do they really eat people?"

Bum nodded seriously and returned to his food. "Yeah, they like kids the best. Those they can't get enough of."

9

ADAM AND HIS FRIENDS WERE TWO HOURS
on the left-hand tunnel before they came to another
fork. This time there were three choices. The cave on
the right curved down. The middle tunnel continued on
a level plane, and the one on the left curved up. They all
had different opinions about which way to go.

"I want to go to the left," Cindy said. "The more we
go up the more chance we have of reaching the surface."

Sally stepped into Cindy's tunnel. She sniffed the air
and frowned. "It stinks in here."

Adam had to agree. "It does smell like there's a dead
animal down that way. I think we should go to the right.
I know it slants down, but there is fresh air blowing out
of it. It could open to the outside."

"No way," Sally said. "We can't go down and we can't go in the direction of dead animals. I say we take the middle route, and you should do what I say because look what happened last time when we listened to Cindy."

"Last time I wanted to go to the right as well," Adam reminded her.

"Only because she whispered the word in your ear," Sally said.

"I would resent that except you just saved my life," Cindy replied.

"And don't you forget it, sister," Sally said.

Adam was undecided. They had been using their second flashlight a long time. The batteries seemed to be holding out pretty well, but they wouldn't last forever. They were all very tired, very thirsty. Each time they paused to rest, they took longer to get up. Adam worried that soon they wouldn't be able to get up at all.

It wasn't just the cool air that made him want to take the downward path. Far away, ever so faintly, he thought he heard the rushing of water. He believed if there was an underground stream, it might eventually lead to the outside. All they would have to do was follow it. Plus they could take care of their thirst. Unfortunately, when he asked the others to listen for the sound of water, they couldn't hear a thing.

"I think you're just so thirsty you're hallucinating," Sally said.

Adam was afraid she might be right, for once. "Are you sure you don't hear it, Cindy?" he asked.

"I'm sorry, Adam," Cindy said. "I don't hear a thing. Plus I just can't see going down. Let's go to the left."

"To the center," Sally insisted.

They were waiting for him to make the final decision. At the moment Adam wished they had another leader. If he made the wrong choice, the chances were he would kill them all. Going against his gut feeling, he nodded toward the middle cave.

"We'll continue this way," he said. "See what happens."

At first there was no change in scenery. The cave continued straight and level. Another hour of thirsty walking went by. They began to lean on one another for support. Adam was still carrying several of the boards from the coffin, and they kept getting heavier and heavier. He was tempted to put them down, but Cindy's flashlight had begun to dim slightly. He tried not to think what it would be like to be trapped, wandering around in the dark. Why, they could come to the edge of a cliff and just walk off it, without realizing it until they were falling.

The middle cave was not without its bad smells, either.

The odor hit them before they saw it.

They found their first dead bat.

They hadn't seen any living ones, of course, but this dead one filled them with dark fear. Adam borrowed the light from Cindy to examine it closer. Other bats had not killed this bat. It was clear that a large creature had torn it open in one swift jerk. There was blood all around it, and the blood, although not fresh, was not dry either.

The bat had sharp tiny teeth.

He wondered if it was a bloodsucker.

"How long ago did it die?" Sally asked, for once standing close to Cindy. Adam sat back from the disgusting remains and frowned.

"Maybe a day," he said.

"It doesn't look like it committed suicide," Sally said.

"No," Adam said, climbing to his feet and handing the flashlight back to Cindy. "I think one of the ape creatures got it." He paused. "Do you still want to go this way, Sally?"

She seemed to be exhausted. Her dark hair clung to the sides of her face like streaks of dirt. Her lips were dry and cracked. Adam's own knee was bleeding slightly from the brush with the troll's spear. But he hadn't told the girls about the wound. It was the last of his worries. Sally shook her head.

"I don't have the energy left to walk back the way we came," she said.

"Do you have the energy to fight what killed the bat?" Cindy asked. She added softly, "We should have gone to the left."

"We shouldn't have come into the cave at all," Sally snapped. "This wasn't my brilliant idea." Yet she didn't have the strength to continue arguing. She hung her head wearily, looking at the bat once more. "You decide, Adam. I can't."

He shook his head. "We've already decided. We can only go forward."

Forward quickly got more gruesome. Spider webs appeared. Not the annoying little things they saw around their yards or garages from time to time. These were massive webs. They spanned the width of the cave. To keep going, Adam had to remove his shirt to swipe at them. And sometimes the spiders would come running out and snap at them with tiny black claws and greasy red eyes. They saw one spider that was as large as a small rabbit. But it ran away when Adam threw a rock at it.

The temperature increased. Thirst and exhaustion were all they knew. Adam tried to figure out what time it was but was unable to focus long enough. It felt as if they had been trapped in the cave for weeks. Briefly he wondered if

Watch had talked to his parents, if his mom and dad were planning his funeral. At least they wouldn't have to pay for a coffin, he thought. The entire cave could be his tomb.

They stumbled upon another two dead bats. Adam knelt to examine them. They didn't smell as bad as the first one because their blood was fresher. They had been killed in exactly the same way as the first one. The girls waited anxiously for his opinion. He was afraid to give it.

"Well?" Sally said impatiently.

"I think these bats died in the last two hours," he said.

"Did they die here?" Cindy asked.

"Looks like it," Adam said, standing back up.

Cindy's voice cracked as she spoke. "That means one of those creatures was just here."

"What it really means is one of those creatures is not far from here," Sally said.

"But we haven't heard it in a while," Adam said.

Sally's eyes shifted from side to side. "I've been hearing something. Faint steps that pause when we pause. And I've felt eyes on me. You know what it's like when someone's staring at you behind your back. You can feel it. Well, something is staring at us."

"You're imagining it," Cindy said quickly.

Sally pointed at the dead bats. "Am I imagining that? I'm telling you the truth, I think we've been followed for a while."

"Why didn't you say something earlier?" Adam asked.

"What good would it do?" Sally asked.

Adam glanced up and down the tunnel, using the beam of the flashlight to pierce the darkness. Beyond the light's range there was only darkness and spiders and probably more dead bats.

"If it is following us," he said, "and it hasn't attacked yet, that might mean it doesn't want to attack."

"That's wishful thinking," Sally said. She also looked around and then shivered, although she seemed ready to fall over from heat exhaustion. "But I suppose that's the best kind of thinking we can have right now."

Cindy wrinkled her nose at the bloody bats. "One thing's for sure—the bat killer is not a vegetarian."

Sally nodded grimly. "It probably doesn't even like ice cream."

They continued on. The air was so dry now it was hard to swallow. Another odor floated through the air. It had probably always been there, but they had just gotten used to it. Now it was too strong to ignore. They were definitely approaching some kind of active volcanic area. Tiny black cinders floated in the air before them and caught in their hair. The odor and the cinders made it harder to breathe. They were all coughing.

Then the black cloud came.

They had seen dead bats, but no live ones, and that

had made Adam wonder. Soon he would wonder no more. They were taking a short rest when Adam heard a faint flapping above them. He was the first to hear it. As the sound grew louder, it took on a peculiar humming quality. For a moment he wondered if he was listening to a swarm of bees. The girls turned to him.

"What's that?" Sally asked nervously.

Adam jumped up and shone his flashlight in the direction of the sound. Actually, it was coming from behind them, from the length of the tunnel they had just walked. At first he couldn't see anything except the remains of the spider webs they had pushed through. But then all of a sudden the webs began to shake violently. One huge spider, hanging on to what was left of its broken home, turned to shreds in midair. Something *new* was pushing through the webs. Something with several thousand black wings and a million pairs of beady red eyes.

A swarm of bats was coming.

Coming right toward them.

"Run!" Adam shouted, pushing the girls in front of him.

They ran as fast as they could, but they were no match for winged creatures. The bats were on them in a minute and the horror of it was beyond imagining. They were in their hair, under their shirts, pecking at their ears and fingers. Adam felt the claws of a bat land on his closed eyes. He brushed it away but two took its place. He remembered the tiny sharp teeth of the dead bats and a second later he felt them as several bats tried to bite into his skin. He wanted to scream louder than he had ever screamed in his entire life, but he was afraid a bat would fly into his mouth.

The bats were thirsty. They wanted blood.

What a way to die. Such a horrible death.

Yet all was not lost. Adam accidentally opened one eye and caught a faint glimpse of a strange red light fifty feet ahead. It flashed out from a narrow crack in the wall of the cave. Curiously enough, there were no bats around this light. That was enough for Adam. He grabbed the girls' arms as they continued to wave them to keep from being eaten alive.

"I see a way out!" he shouted. "Come with me!"

He pulled the stumbling girls after him. The bats followed, of course, since they were thirsty little devils. Yet as they moved within ten feet of the smoldering orange crack in the wall, the bats veered away. Adam assumed they didn't like the smell, or else the wicked red light disturbed them. He squeezed through the crack first, pulling the girls in behind him.

They took a second to get their bearings.

They were standing in a huge volcanic chamber.

10

SPOOKSVILLE'S LARGEST GROCERY STORE was called Fred's Foods. Fred himself was a bagger at the store—he had been for thirty years. He owned the place but couldn't figure out how to work the cash registers or do anything else useful. So he bagged groceries and helped people out to their cars. It was lucky for Fred that he had hired an assistant manager with half a brain, or else the place would have closed down ages ago.

Watch and Bum found Ms. Ann Templeton in the produce department, knocking lightly on watermelons. She wore an expensive white pantsuit, shiny black shoes, and exquisite diamond earrings. Her long black hair was curly; it reached almost to her waist. Her face, as she glanced over at them and smiled, was as beautiful as always, and as pale. She was either an angel from heaven, or a ghost from a much lower place. Her dark eyes shone with wicked amusement. She couldn't have been more than thirty years old.

"Watch and Bum," she said in her soft yet powerful voice. "Have you come to help carry my groceries to my car? I could use some help this fine evening. I think poor old Fred has already left for the day."

Bum bowed slightly. "I wouldn't mind helping you with your food, ma'am, if you could spare me a loaf of bread or two."

"I will give you a can of tuna," Ms. Templeton said. She studied him and frowned at his appearance. "I think you could use some fish. Your skin looks terrible."

"It's the sleeping outdoors every night that does it," Bum said.

"There are worse places to sleep, I suppose." She returned to knocking on watermelons. "Looking for your friends, Watch?"

Watch almost jumped out of his socks. "Yeah. How did you know they were missing?"

"Nothing happens in Spooksville that I don't know about. Isn't that true, Bum?"

"Yeah, ma'am. No one puts anything past you."

Ms. Templeton continued. "Your friends somehow managed to sneak into my basement, Watch. I should say it was one of my *lower* basements, not the best way to enter my castle, if you're a human being. I am sorry to say that they were not given the most hospitable welcome."

"What happened?" Watch asked, worried.

"A couple of my boys tried to have them for dinner." Ms. Templeton smiled. "It is so hard to find good help these days. I don't know what the world's coming to."

Watch gulped. "Are they dead?"

Ms. Templeton chuckled. "Heavens no. Thanks to Adam, they escaped. I'm sure they're still wandering around down there somewhere, unless the bats or Hyeets have eaten them."

Watch took a step forward. "Can you help me rescue them?" He added, "I'll help carry your groceries out to your car for the next two months."

Ms. Templeton threw her head back and laughed. "If I help you that will spoil all the fun. Watch, you wouldn't want that. It wouldn't be fair to them."

"But you said it yourself, they might die."

Ms. Templeton shrugged. "Lots of people die in this town. I can't be responsible for all of them." She picked up a plump watermelon. "Now this one looks ripe."

"But I thought you liked Adam," Watch protested.

"What made you think that?" Ms. Templeton asked.

"I don't know," Watch said. "He likes you."

She glanced over. "Really?"

Watch nodded. "Yeah. He thinks you're real pretty. It drives Sally crazy."

Ms. Templeton was amused. "It's fun to see Sally lose her temper. She reminds me of myself when I was young." She paused. "Do you know what I used to do when I was your age, Watch? Just for fun?"

Bum shook his head. "I remember."

"I'm sure you do," she said. "And I'm sure you're glad I never did it to you. In those days, Watch, I was fond of hiking in the caves with several of the kids at school. I would dare them to join me, usually boys who made fun of my family. Then when we were a mile or two underground, I would make all their flashlights fail. It would scare them so bad they would start crying and screaming for help. Just like little babies."

"Would you help them?" Watch asked.

Ms. Templeton set the watermelon in her cart. "Sometimes, but not often. I think a lot of those kids are still down there, in the bellies of the Hyeets." She laughed when she saw Watch's confused expression. "All right, since Adam thinks I'm so pretty, I will give you a couple of hints that might help you rescue them."

Watch looked around for pen and paper. "Do I need to take notes?"

"No, just listen," Ms. Templeton said. "The entrance to the cave closed up on Adam and his friends, right?"

"Right," Watch said. "For no reason."

She shook her head. "There was a reason. The Haunted Cave is sensitive. It does what you tell it. Someone must have accidentally told the cave to close."

"No," Watch disagreed. "No one said anything about—"

But then he stopped, remembering the words Cindy had shouted at Sally. Even though he had been standing outside the cave, he had heard them loud and clear.

Yeah, but you've got a poison tongue. I wish for just once you would shut up. That you would close your mouth, shut it tight . . .

Watch continued. "Cindy did say something about shutting tight. She was talking about Sally's mouth, but the cave did start to close right then."

"That's it," Ms. Templeton said. "The cave thought you wanted it to close up. So it did."

"Then all we have to do is return to the entrance and command it to open?" Watch asked.

"That works some of the time," she said thoughtfully. "But a tribe of Native Americans lived here long before Europeans came, and the cave is more receptive to their language. They were called the Reeksvars. They named the Hyeets and many other strange creatures in this area. Their word for open was *Bela*. Their word for close was *Nela*. It's always good to know how to close whatever you happen to open. If you shout *Bela* to the cave, it will open right away." She paused. "But your friends are nowhere near that entrance by the reservoir. They've been walking all night. If you go there, you won't find them."

Watch felt frustrated. "Is there another way into the cave?"

Ms. Templeton mocked him. "You can always try my lower basement. But I can't guarantee you'll make it past my boys. Adam and his friends got them all riled up. I'm going to have to buy them a dozen boxes of Ritz crackers just to calm them down."

"They like crackers?" Watch asked, confused about exactly who or what her *boys* were.

"Yes," she said. "Very much, with snails and spiders. But to return to your question, there are several entrances to the cave. You just have to know how to find them." She leaned over and spoke softly in his ear. "I will give you one more hint, Watch. The wells in this town run deep. The waters run cold. It is hot where your friends now walk, but soon they will be able to soothe their thirst. If they're lucky."

Watch brightened. "Then they are alive."

Ms. Templeton stood back up and nodded. "They're alive for now. But the night is far from over. The Hyeets hunt at night. If they run into one, there's no telling what will happen."

"But I don't understand your hint," Watch said. "I still don't know how to get to them."

She patted him on the head. "That's your problem." She handed Bum a can of tuna. "Good night, Bum. Good night, Watch. You can help me with my groceries next time. I will remember your promise. And you remember me, whenever you are eager for strange dreams or exciting adventures."

"Have a fine evening, ma'am," Bum said, holding on to the can of tuna as if it were a rose from a girlfriend. He grabbed Watch by the arm as Ms. Templeton disappeared around another aisle. "I heard what she said to you. You don't want to push her. Her moods are quick to change. She might put a curse on you. She told us more than I thought she would."

"Do you know how we can reach Adam and the others?" Watch asked.

Bum nodded. "Based on what she said, I have an idea."

11

THE CHAMBER WAS AS WIDE AND HIGH AS A high-school auditorium. There was not one but a half-dozen pools of glowing lava spread about the stone room. Steam rose from the glowing liquid rock, gathering near the ceiling of the chamber, forming a shimmering cloud of sparks and fumes. Every few seconds a miniature geyser would spurt up from one of the molten pools and splash the surrounding black rock. The place was as hot as an oven. They were able to see clearly without their flashlight, but the sober red glow had a strange effect on them. It was as if they had died and gone to an evil place. Sally said it for all of them when she spoke next.

"I hope there are no devils in here," she said.

"I don't believe in devils," Cindy said quickly.

"I would think you would believe in everything after tonight," Sally said, wiping at a bloody scratch on her face. "I'm just happy we got away from those bats. I think they were vampires."

"Spooksville would have no other kind," Adam agreed, also wiping at his face and arms. He had a dozen small scratches, but none were serious. The bats had been the hardest on Cindy. She had several big bites in her left ear. Adam had to admire her. The bites were bleeding but she wasn't complaining.

Although the light from the lava pits was reassuring, the fumes in the place made it hard to breathe. They were pretty much constantly coughing, and their thirst was a real problem now. After the bat attack, they felt even more dehydrated. Adam noticed the girls beginning to wobble on their feet. He was having trouble focusing his own eyes. Plus he was beginning to get a headache. He nodded at the chamber.

"Let's explore this place quickly," he said. "But if we don't find anything that can help us, then we have to go back into the cave."

"But the bats are in the cave," Sally protested.

"We have no choice," Adam said. "Besides they might have flown off. We might not see them again."

"If they catch us away from here," Cindy said, "we're dead."

"You took the words right out of my mouth," Sally said.

They had been exploring the chamber only a couple of minutes when they found a strange set of four lines on the far wall. They made the shape of a large doorlike rectangle, and were etched into the rock. The bottom line started two feet above the floor and ran parallel to it. The top had to be twelve feet above them. It was a big door, perhaps for huge creatures to go in and out. But it wasn't really a door, just lines on a wall. Like a caveman's drawing. They exchanged puzzled glances.

"Somebody cut these into the rock," Adam said.

"What for?" Sally asked.

"Your guess is as good as mine," Adam said.

Sally reached out and touched the sharp-edged grooves. They were about two inches deep, straight, and without flaws. The surrounding volcanic stone was hard. It would have taken a powerful instrument to cut the lines.

"The person who drew these was not just doodling," Sally said. "This could be a door of some kind. A portal to another place."

"But it has no hinges," Cindy said. "No doorknob."

"Interdimensional portals don't need hinges or door-knobs," Sally said. "Adam and I have had experience with this kind of thing before. When we passed through the Secret Path."

Adam nodded. "But that portal took us into a night-mare world. I wonder if this doorway would do the same—if we knew how to open it."

Cindy spoke with feeling. "We already are in a night-mare world. If we can open it, then we should open it." She coughed, choked actually. Her voice came out weak and dry. "I need water real bad."

"I wouldn't mind a tall glass of ginger ale myself," Sally said. She glanced at Adam. "Can you think of any special spells to open this door?"

Adam shook his head. "With the Secret Path, we just had to walk backward into the tombstone to make it work."

"Not really," Sally said. "First we had to trek all over town in a certain order." She paused. "But if you want to try walking backward into the thing, I'm all for it."

Together, the three of them tried the technique that had worked so well in the graveyard. But they just ended up bumping their heads on the hard stone wall. Adam was not enthusiastic about experimenting any more.

"We're dripping sweat even when we stand still," he

said. "We're going to lose what water our bodies have left if we don't get out of here."

"But that tunnel in the cave was leading us nowhere," Sally protested. "We have to give this a chance."

"What should we do?" Adam asked simply.

Sally threw up her arms. "I don't know. Let me fool with it for a bit. You guys go sit closer to the cave, where it's cooler. Please, Adam, give me at least ten minutes."

"No more," Adam warned. "You'll pass out if you stay any longer." He surveyed the bubbling pools as he wiped the sweat from his face. "I wonder if the ape creatures ever come here?"

It was an interesting question to ask.

Perhaps it was the wrong question.

Adam rested with Cindy by the crack in the cave wall that led into the volcanic chamber. They sat outside, on the cave side. There the temperature was still warm, but at least it wasn't blasting like a furnace. They stared at each other, probably wondering which one of them looked worse. Cindy's blond hair was covered with black soot. The blood from her ear had spilled onto her white blouse. Her lips were cracked and starting to bleed. Her eyes were so weary, she looked as if she hadn't slept in days.

"Are we going to get out of here?" she asked after a minute of silence.

Adam sighed. "I don't know. There could be an exit just around the next curve, or the cave tunnels could go on for another ten miles. But we've been walking under Spooksville for the last few hours, and I can't imagine that the caves run under the ocean. For that reason, I think we're going to reach the end of the road, one way or the other."

"You mean the cave might just end in a wall?" Cindy asked.

"Or it might end in someone's backyard. It's possible."

Cindy was doubtful. "But we don't know of anyone who has a cave opening in their backyard."

Adam nodded reluctantly. "That's true. If the cave does have an exit inside the city, then it's where no one knows about it."

Cindy shook her head sadly, fingering the flashlight. They didn't need it turned on here. But the moment they left this area it would be their only source of illumination. Adam thought the batteries couldn't last more than another hour.

"This is all my fault," she said quietly. "I forced us into this cave."

"You didn't force me. I wanted to come."

Cindy smiled faintly. "That's nice of you to say,

Adam, but I think I forced you more than anyone. I just assumed you'd come. And you did." She paused. "Why?"

He shrugged. "It sounded like an interesting adventure."

"But you've had plenty of those since you moved here." She paused again. "Did you come because you thought I'd think you were a coward if you didn't?"

"No," he said. Then he added, "Maybe."

Cindy laughed softly. "I could never think that. You're the bravest boy I've ever met."

"Really?" That was nice to hear.

Cindy touched his knee. "Of course. Who else our age would swim with sharks and fight with ghosts and wrestle with trolls?"

"Sally."

Cindy giggled. "Sally's weird. I don't really hate her, you know. I just love to tease her. She has so many buttons, and I can't stop pushing them."

"I think she cares about you, too. You saw the way she risked her life to save you from that troll's spear?"

Cindy nodded. "I just hope I don't need to be saved again."

It may have been the wrong thing to say.

Especially considering where they were sitting.

Adam didn't know exactly what happened next.

The cave around them was black, of course. Everything underground was black. But it seemed as if for a moment a deeper blackness rose up from some hidden depths. The shadow came from one side, and it swiftly took on a vague shape. Adam saw a hairy face, yellow teeth, weird eyes—yet it was all a blur. Before he could react, even shout, the shadow fell on Cindy. It covered her in darkness and then quickly pulled back into the black. Cindy wasn't given a chance to scream. Adam wasn't given a chance to save her.

She was just gone.

The monster had her.

12

BUM KNEW ABOUT A WELL LOCATED NOT far from the beach. He believed it was one of the wells Ann Templeton had been referring to. Watch had never heard of the place, and he knew the town inside and out. Or at least he thought he did. But Bum explained why he had never seen it before.

"It's located in an old woman's backyard," Bum said. "Her name's Mrs. Robinson. She never leaves her house. When her husband died ten years ago, she didn't even go to his funeral. A young man brings her groceries. She hasn't been out of her house in forty years. She has that disease where she's afraid to go outside. But that's understandable in this town. A lot of senior citizens have it. Anyway, I once rented a room from her, so I know her pretty well. She's not a bad person, although she's addicted to black-and-white reruns on TV. I used to have to watch them every night, just to get to the news. While I lived there, we used to get all our water from her backyard well."

"But why do you think it's one of the wells Ms. Templeton was talking about?" Watch asked.

"Because I can't think of any other private well in town. Also, it's very deep. You have to lower your bucket way down to get any water. I used to get calluses on my hands trying to get a drink. The water you do get is ice cold. Remember how the witch mentioned the cold."

Watch scratched his head. "Is Ann Templeton really a witch? She seems so nice."

"Get on her bad side and you'll see how nice she is. I think the best way to understand her is to know that she does whatever amuses her. She has the power to do that. If it strikes her fancy, she'll save you from a thousand enemies. But if she's in a dark mood, she'll feed you to her boys."

"Who are her boys?" Watch asked

"You mean *what* are her boys. I don't want to talk about them tonight. We have enough problems." Bum pulled Watch down the street. "We have to hurry to

Mrs. Robinson's house. She does stay up late with her TV, but it's already two in the morning."

They reached the house twenty minutes later. It was an old wooden affair that stared out at the rock jetty and the burned-down lighthouse. Two stories tall, with a steeply pitched tar-paper roof, it didn't look as if it had been painted in the last two decades. Watch wondered how many other old people there were in Spooksville who never left their houses. Who just peered out from between their curtains and were terrified of the horrors that walked outside. Actually, Watch was amazed that anyone lived long enough in Spooksville to get old. He couldn't imagine he would last past his twenties. The thought didn't bother him, though. Not right now.

"You stay here on the sidewalk," Bum instructed. "It's better if I talk to her alone. She gets jittery around strangers. Last week a brand-new letter carrier tried to deliver her mail and she blew a hole in his mail bag with her shotgun."

"She has a shotgun?" Watch asked, amazed.

"Yeah, and she's a crack shot. Just give me a minute with her. She's proud of her well. If I tell her I have a friend who's just dying to taste the water from it, she'll let us run all over her backyard."

Bum was gone several minutes. Watch could see him

talking to someone on the front porch of the house, but with the shadows he couldn't tell who it was. When Bum returned, he was grinning.

"We can fool with her well all we want," Bum said. Watch noticed he had a flashlight in his hands and a coil of rope. The old woman must have given him the stuff. Bum didn't have a penny to his name, but whatever he needed just came to him. Watch wondered if Bum had powers of his own.

"I want to thank you for helping me rescue my friends," Watch said as they hurried around to the back of the house. Bum waved his hand.

"No problem," he said. "I like your friends."

"But you were ready to let them die when I first spoke to you."

Bum chuckled. "I was just hungry. When I haven't eaten in a couple of days, I never feel like rescuing anyone."

The well was nicely constructed. Built of gray bricks and a few white painted boards, it stood in the center of the backyard like a prized plant. It had a small roof over it, from which hung a rope, a pail, and a lowering winch. Watch wasn't sure what Bum had planned, but was sure it would be dangerous.

"You're not going to lower me down there, are

you?" Watch asked, when he saw Bum tying the extra rope onto one of the well's support poles. The question amused Bum.

"They're your friends," he said. "And better you than me."

Watch stared down into the black well. "How far down before I reach water?"

"At least two hundred feet."

"Can you lower me that far?"

"Lowering you is no problem. It's pulling you back up that'll be hard. I just hope my back doesn't give out."

Watch took Bum's flashlight and shone it down the well. Still, he couldn't see anything except pure blackness. But ever so faintly he did hear gurgling water. It sounded as if it was moving, an underground river.

"What if there's no room to breathe down there?" he asked. "To stand up?"

Bum nodded. "I thought of that. You might just end up in a cold pool, with no way out. If you do, shout for me to pull you back up."

Watch nodded as he swung a leg up onto the edge of the well. "Should I hang on to both the new rope and the old pail rope as I go down?" he asked.

"Yes," Bum said. "It'll decrease your chances that either of the ropes will break. You know, Watch, I have to admire your courage. If my friends were trapped down there, I wouldn't try to rescue them. Not that I have many friends."

"Does that mean if you can't pull me up, I'm doomed?"

"Exactly," Bum said cheerfully, slapping him on the back. "But I wish you the best of luck anyway."

Watch grabbed hold of both ropes. He kept the flashlight on and tucked it in his belt. He just hoped his glasses didn't fall off.

"Let's get this over with," he said.

Bum began to lower him down the deep shaft. Yet Watch didn't only depend on Bum's strength for support. The well was narrow. As he descended, he wedged himself against the opposite sides of the circular wall—his upper back jammed on one side, his feet on the other. Above, he could see Bum's face growing smaller and smaller. Soon it was just a dark dot against a black sky. Watch gripped the ropes tightly. He kept waiting for the feel of the water but it never came.

Yet the sound of the gurgling water grew louder. When Bum had become all but invisible, Watch felt a faint spray on his face. He stopped his descent and carefully pulled his flashlight from his belt. The well did not end in just water, but in a small air space. Panning around with the beam, he saw that two feet more and he would have burst free of the shaft, which now was dug out of bedrock. For the first time he hung with all his weight on the end of the two ropes and tried to peer around the edge of the shaft. What he needed to know was if there was only water below him. If there was no bedrock to lower himself on, he would have to abandon his rescue efforts.

And leave his friends to the Hyeets.

A moment later he saw that the well didn't draw its water from a pool. The black liquid twenty feet below him was definitely moving. If he wasn't messed up on his directions, it seemed to be flowing toward the ocean.

Watch found that interesting.

Unfortunately, as he stuck his head under the edge of the shaft, he could see no place to swim to. The underground river flowed out of one wall of blackness, and disappeared into another. It might reappear in an open space, but he couldn't drop down and take that chance. Swimming underwater and underground with the icy river, with nothing to breathe, he would drown in minutes.

A wave of sorrow swept over Watch then. It was rare that he allowed himself to experience any powerful emotion, but he had known Sally a long time. And in the last couple of weeks he had come to admire Adam a great deal. Plus Cindy was his friend as well. To lose all three of them at once would be horrible. He knew he needed to shout for Bum to pull him back up because there was nothing he could do. But Watch hesitated, straining to think of some way he could help his friends even if he couldn't see them.

But nothing came to Watch.

"Bum!" he shouted reluctantly. "Pull me up!"

The tension on both ropes increased. Bum was pulling with all his strength. Too bad he was the town bum instead of the physical education teacher. He wasn't that strong. Watch had to aid Bum's efforts by trying to crawl up the shaft, his upper back still jammed against one wall, his feet against the other. The problem was he was tired from the descent, and his strength was giving out, faster than he could have imagined. He tried to rest for brief moments by letting all his weight rest on the ropes, but Bum must have been tiring quickly also. When Watch did relax, he ended up slipping back down several feet.

This went on for over twenty minutes. At the end of that time, the top of the well was still far away. Watch wasn't sure what to do. He was breathing hard and his arms and legs and back ached terribly. He paused to take another quick break, to gather his strength. As he did so he let all his weight hang on the ropes.

Disaster struck quickly and without warning.

The ropes gave way and Watch fell.

There was nothing to do. He tried grasping at the walls of the shaft, but they slipped from his fingers. The overhead circle of sky shrank. Watch felt the cold air on his face just before the freezing water slapped his entire body.

Watch went under. He went down, into blackness.

He struggled frantically. Trying to reach a surface he couldn't see.

For a moment his head broke the surface.

He heard Bum shout from far overhead.

"I'm soooorrrryyyyy!"

Then the current of the underground river gripped Watch and carried him against the far black wall and under the water once more. Where there was no light, and no air. He fought for a surface that didn't exist. The cold was crushing, his panic shattering. He was in a liquid tomb and there was absolutely no way out.

13

"WE HAVE TO SAVE HER," ADAM WAS SAYing. "We can do it."

"How?" Sally asked. "Cindy had our only working flashlight. It went when she went. We can't walk a hundred feet in this dark."

"What about the first flashlight? There was still a little juice left in it."

"There's none now. I tried it a minute ago. The light's dead."

"Let me see it," Adam demanded. They were standing just outside the volcanic chamber, on the exact spot where Cindy had been swiped. Sally handed over the flashlight, and Adam flipped the switch and pointed it around the cave. He couldn't see a thing. "Why would it stop working?" he muttered.

"I may have accidentally turned it on while it was in my back pocket," Sally said. "It doesn't matter. It wouldn't have lasted five minutes."

Adam paced restlessly. "It does matter. We need only five minutes to save her."

"Adam—" Sally tried to speak.

He threw up his arms in frustration. "We were just sitting here talking and it took her. It moved so fast. I didn't even get a chance to grab her arm, to fight for her."

"You can't blame yourself," Sally said.

"Then who am I supposed to blame? I tell you, we have to go after her. We have to go now."

"But we won't be able to see where we're going," Sally protested.

"It doesn't matter. We can feel our way along the walls of the cave."

"That won't work for long. There're forks and side tunnels in this cave. We'll just end up lost in the dark."

"Then what do you think we should do?"

Sally hesitated. "Nothing."

Adam was exasperated. "We can't do anything! It'll kill her!"

Sally put her hand on his shoulder and spoke carefully.

"Adam, it's a big hairy monster. I know this isn't easy to hear, but it's probably already killed her. If we try to save Cindy, it will just kill us."

Adam was angry. "You just don't like her. You're jealous of her. You don't care if it eats her. In fact, you're probably happy it grabbed her."

Sally spoke patiently. "Earlier tonight I risked my life to save Cindy. I'm sure you haven't forgotten. Yeah, sure, I yell at her every five minutes. But that doesn't mean I don't like her. I yell at you all the time. If I thought there was a chance we could rescue her, I'd take that chance. But there's no hope. We don't even know where it took her."

Adam pointed down the cave, in the direction they hadn't gone yet. "They went that way. I'm going that way. I don't care what you say."

"You'll lose your way in a few minutes," Sally said.

Adam looked down at his pile of boards. "Maybe not. Dipped in lava, these boards could work as torches. If we get them burning bright enough, we might even be able to use them as weapons. Most animals are afraid of fire. I bet this creature is, too."

Sally considered the idea. "The wood won't burn for long."

"It may not have taken her far." Adam paused and added reluctantly, "If it's that hungry."

Sally glanced into the volcanic chamber, then nodded wearily. "If you want to try, I'll go with you. There's no use in staying here anyway. I'm never going to get that magic door to open. If it is a door."

They gathered together their boards. Approaching the boiling pools, they had no trouble soaking the tips of the boards with molten lava. Tiny flames flared around the edges of the lava lumps, but the sticks didn't burst into flames, which was good. The torches didn't give off much light, but it appeared they'd last longer than a few minutes. They made only two torches. They figured they could always light the other sticks and transfer the lava when the first boards had burned down.

They set off at a brisk walk. They were fortunate the creature had left huge tracks in the dirt floor, because they soon came to another fork in the tunnel. The thing had gone to the right so they went to the right. Based on its foot size, Adam figured the creature must be eight feet tall. In the dismal red glow of their torches, he searched for signs of Cindy's blood on the cave floor. He prayed the whole time. If he saw her blood, he knew he would lose all hope.

They reached another fork. This time the creature had veered to the left. Making the turn, they felt a sudden drop in temperature. The change was remarkable.

But they were soon given a reason for the coolness. Ten minutes along this new path and they came to a cold black river. This last portion of cave had widened considerably. The river flowed along the right side, hugging the wall. They were desperate to save their friend, but they both took a moment to fall to their knees to take a drink. Adam swallowed so much cold water so quickly his tongue momentarily froze and he had trouble speaking. Sally gulped away beside him.

"I never thought water could taste so good," she mumbled. "This is better than my morning coffee."

Adam grunted. "Good. Hmm."

"I wonder where this river leads?"

Adam looked around. It led in the direction the creature had taken Cindy. He climbed back to his feet, anxious to resume the hunt. He grabbed his dull red torch and worked his tongue in his mouth.

"We'll see," he said. "Let's go."

But then Sally suddenly grabbed his arm.

"Adam!" she screamed, pointing. "A horrible fish monster is coming out of the river! Look!"

Adam turned to see a big white object struggling in the stream. It seemed to have emerged from just under the far wall. Since their torches gave off as much light as a fat cigar, neither of them could make out its shape right away. But it seemed—Adam stopped and rubbed his eyes—to be wearing glasses.

"Watch?" Adam gasped. "Is that you?"

The terrible monster grabbed the bank of the river and peered up at them through thick lenses. It was gasping for breath and shivering uncontrollably.

"Yeah, it's me," he whispered. "Is that you, Adam?"

"Yeah. Sally and I are both here. I'll give you a hand." They pulled Watch from the water. He was as cold as a Popsicle. He couldn't even stand at first, he was so numb. He lay on the floor of the cave, trying to catch his breath and wiping the water off his glasses.

"I'm glad these didn't fall off," he said. "Can't see a thing without them."

Adam and Sally knelt by his side. They tried rubbing his arms and legs to restore his circulation. His shivering began to lessen.

"But where did you come from?" Adam asked.

Watch sat up with effort. "Mrs. Robinson's backyard," he said.

"Who's Mrs. Robinson?" Adam asked.

Sally made a face. "I know her. She's a creepy old woman who never leaves her house. Ten years ago she poisoned her husband and didn't even have the decency to attend his funeral."

"I don't know about that," Watch said. "But she's got a deep well in the middle of her backyard." Watch went on to give them a brief explanation of what he had done since they last saw him. He even related what the witch had said. Adam found it all very fascinating, but he was still anxious to go after Cindy. He helped Watch to his feet.

"How long were you underwater?" Adam asked.

Watch coughed. "Just a couple of minutes. But it was a long two minutes."

Adam noticed he was carrying a flashlight. "Does your light work?"

Watch tried it. Nothing. "I guess the water got to the batteries."

"You wouldn't happen to have a high-powered pistol in your pocket?" Sally asked.

"No." Watch blinked. "Where's Cindy?"

"An ape creature grabbed her," Adam explained. "It's been about twenty minutes since she disappeared." He pointed to the floor. "We're following these tracks. Are you strong enough to walk?"

Watch nodded. "I think it would warm me up. But I have to warn you guys about these creatures. They're called Hyeets and they're supposed to take no prisoners."

"Then we'd better hurry," Adam said. "Come on."

14

THE CAVE FORKED ANOTHER THREE TIMES, but the footprints remained clear. Fifteen minutes after finding Watch, Adam heard sounds up ahead. He raised his hand, cautioning the others to slow their pace. He could hear a faint growling—that was clear enough. But he also thought he heard Cindy's voice.

"What's going on here?" he whispered aloud.

"Maybe they're saying grace together before dinner," Sally suggested. "Maybe Cindy doesn't realize she is the main course."

"I have water in my ears," Watch apologized. "I can't hear anything."

"Maybe you two should wait here," Adam said. "There's no sense in all of us being killed."

"Nonsense," Sally said. "If we have to fight the monster, we'll fight it together. That way we might stand a chance."

Adam agreed with her logic. They crept forward cautiously. Another hundred feet and it was clear both Cindy and the Hyeet were making noise. The weird thing was, Cindy didn't act hysterical.

They reached another turn. Adam made them stop.

Cindy and the Hyeet appeared to be just around the corner.

"This is it," Adam whispered. "We fight to the death."

"We don't take prisoners either," Sally agreed.

"I can't believe I let myself get mixed up in this," Watch remarked.

They raised their torches and ran around the corner.

They stopped dead in their tracks.

Cindy looked over at them. "Hi, guys. Glad you could make it."

The Hyeet, the loathsome evil monster, was indeed eight feet tall. Clearly it was a cross between a man and an ape—the fabled missing link. Except for around its eyes, nose, and mouth, it was covered with black hair. Its nose was wide; the nostrils flared as it drew in hungry breaths. It had massive hands, large feet. But it was its eyes that were the most peculiar. They were bigger than those of a human, but were an eerie green. They seemed to glow in the dark. Whirling at the sudden intrusion of three small humans, it looked as if its eyes might burst from its head. It scampered backward and hugged its midsection with its hands. Cindy had been sitting down with her back to a wall, but she jumped to her feet and held up her own hands.

"Don't scare it," she pleaded.

"Don't scare it?" Sally asked. "We're here to kill it."

Cindy shook her head. "No. We had it all wrong. This creature means us no harm. In fact, I think it's more afraid of us than we are of it."

"If that's true," Adam said—although he was relieved to see Cindy all in one piece—"why did it grab you and carry you off?"

He asked the question angrily because he couldn't help noticing that their only working flashlight lay broken on the ground. Perhaps it had fallen from her hands while she was being carried by the creature. Perhaps the light had scared the creature, and it had broken it deliberately. It didn't really matter, the flashlight wasn't going to work anymore. The batteries themselves appeared damaged.

"Because it's desperate," Cindy said. "I think it needs our help."

"Our help with what?" Sally asked. "Preparing vampire bats for dinner?"

Cindy glanced at the creature, which continued to hug the far wall. Adam noticed that it was trembling. It may even have been weeping; its green eyes were moist. It was no longer growling, now it was whimpering. And it looked to Cindy to defend it, even though it was five times her size.

"I don't know what it needs," Cindy said. "It's been trying to communicate with me using sign language."

Sally frowned "Is it deaf?"

Cindy was annoyed. "No. But it doesn't speak English."

"Well, if it wants to live in Spooksville it should learn," Sally said.

Adam lowered his torch. He'd had experience talking to strange creatures. Why, the previous week he had talked down a ghost from an astral rage. He thought he might be able to handle the Hyeet. As he took a step toward it, it pushed itself against the wall.

"We won't hurt you," he said in a gentle voice. "We want to help you. We want you to help us. What is it you need?" Adam pointed at it and smiled. "You," he said again.

The Hyeet seemed to relax slightly. It gestured to them with one of its hairy paws. "Rrrrlllloooo," it said.

Sally glanced at Watch. "Did the witch teach you what that meant?"

"She only taught me two words in Reeksvar," Watch replied. "One for *open*, the other for *close*."

"Reeksvars," Adam said to the creature, nodding his head "Reeksvars?"

The creature nodded "Reekssss," it said.

"I think we're making progress," Adam remarked.

"You could have fooled me," Sally said. "Find out what the beast wants and ask it the way out of here. Then I'll be impressed."

"I have received the impression this creature is alone here in these caves," Cindy said. "The way it hugs itself, and shakes back and forth, it's like it has lost all its friends and family. Once it started communicating with me, it got all excited."

"You could tell all that by its gestures?" Adam asked, impressed.

Cindy shook her head. "I think it can understand more of what we're saying than we can understand of what it's saying." She paused. "I wonder if it can read our minds. Not clearly, I mean, but that it can pick up on the sense of what we're saying."

"It might simply be smarter than we are," Watch said.

"Speak for yourself," Sally said.

"If it has lost its friends," Adam said. "We have to ask ourselves where it lost them?"

"The bats might have got them," Cindy suggested.

"I don't think so," Adam said. "Bats and spiders probably don't bother the Hyeet one bit. It is used to living underground." He glanced at Sally. "Do you have any theories on where the other Hyeets might have gone?"

Realization dawned on Sally. "Through the mysterious doorway!" she exclaimed. Then she paused. "Wait a second. Why would this one have been left behind? And even if it was left behind, why would it be unable to open the door by itself?"

"There could be a thousand answers to those questions," Adam said. "But it's curious Ms. Templeton taught Watch the two words that she did. You say she's a witch. I don't know if that's true. But I do know she's got power. Last time I ran into her, she told me something that was going to happen later in the day. And it did happen—I met Bum and passed through the Secret Path. She might be able to see into the future. She might have given Watch those two words because they can be used to control the mysterious doorway."

"It might have been the Reeksvars who cut this doorway into the wall you're talking about," Watch suggested.

"You haven't even seen it," Sally protested.

Watch shrugged. "I'd like to—if it leads out of this place."

"You only just got here," Sally said. "Try being here all night."

"Try watching Bum eat an eight-course meal," Watch replied.

"But even if these special words open the doorway," Sally said. "There's no guarantee that it will lead us back to the surface. From the sound of things, it probably just leads to more Hyeets. I mean no offense, but this guy needs a bath. If I have to live with a whole herd of them for the rest of my life, I will go mental."

Adam nodded. "It's possible we'll help this creature and still be trapped here. But we have to give it a try. Besides, we don't have anything else we can do right now to help ourselves."

Adam turned to the Hyeet and pointed back in the direction of the volcanic chamber. Then he gestured to the lava at the tip of his torch. The creature could very well have been telepathic. The Hyeet seemed to understand. It nodded vigorously. It wanted them to return to that place with it. To Adam's amazement, it offered Adam its big hairy hand.

"I think you've made a friend," Sally said sweetly.

Adam took the Hyeet's hand and looked up into its weird green eyes. They were like large phosphorescent marbles. Adam had to smile; the creature appeared anxious for them to like it. The Hyeet tried to grin, but the expression ended up resembling something an ape would do while stuffing its face with bananas. The Hyeet accidentally drooled on Adam's arm. Afraid to offend it, Adam didn't immediately wipe off the mess.

"You never know who you're going to meet when you wake up in the morning," Adam said.

15

THE STRANGE RECTANGULAR SHAPE STOOD
etched in the black wall before them. Only twenty feet at
their backs, the lava pools bubbled and hissed. The Hyeet
stared at the shape with something like reverence, mixed
with sorrow. Clearly the creature had come here many
times in the past and gazed hungrily at the markings on
the wall. Adam worried that if the special words Watch
had brought from Ann Templeton failed, the Hyeet would
have a nervous breakdown. It continued to look at them
with such hope. Adam had to take his hand back. The
Hyeet seemed afraid to let go of him. Adam coughed and
cleared his throat. The fumes were as bad as before. Watch
had already told Adam of *Bela*—open—and *Nela*—close.

"We don't know what will happen when we say these words," Adam said. "The rest of you should stand back."

Sally reluctantly agreed. "Just don't let yourself get sucked into a prehistoric zoo," she warned.

A moment later Adam was left alone with the Hyeet before what they hoped was a secret doorway. The others bunched together at the entrance to the chamber. Adam turned and patted the Hyeet on the back. Again the creature tried to smile. It shouldn't have bothered; it just ended up drooling more on Adam.

"Don't eat me if this doesn't work," Adam said.

The Hyeet's eyes moistened again.

It would never do such a thing it seemed to want to say.

Adam turned back to the etchings and took a deep breath.

"Bela!" he shouted.

Nothing happened. For three seconds.

Then many things happened at once.

The wall inside the deeply carved lines began to glow. It took on a blue radiance. The bright color was at complete odds with the sober red of the volcanic pit. The light quickly grew in intensity. Adam had to shield his eyes with his hand. But peeking between his fingers, he saw that not only was the wall glowing, it was becoming transparent. It was as if the black stone was turning to clear glass.

The window began to open.

The scenery that lay beyond was staggering.

Adam glimpsed endless rolling green fields, jungles with trees as tall as mountains, lakes where turtles as large as bears swam. The sky was a brilliant blue. The sun that shone in it seemed twice as big as normal, ten times as bright. Adam briefly wondered if he was looking at the world as it had appeared millions of years ago. Or maybe the doorway opened into another dimension or into another solar system.

Far in the distance he could see other Hyeets.

The Hyeet beside him saw them, too.

The creature squealed with joy and slapped Adam on the back.

Adam almost fell through the magical doorway.

"You go ahead." He gasped, catching the edge of the portal. "Say hi to your friends for me. Enjoy a good meal. I'm sure after eating all those bats, you could use one."

The Hyeet tried to smile one last time. This third effort was as miserable as the first two. But then the creature did the most incredible thing. It put its hand over Adam's heart and worked its wide mouth into a semblance of a human form.

"Adam," it said with feeling.

Adam had to laugh. "Wow."

Then the Hyeet leaped forward, toward the now transparent wall, and was gone. Adam blinked; the Hyeet simply vanished. But Adam thought he caught a glimpse of it running across the wide grass field, yelping in joy, although he wasn't sure. At the moment Adam had other things to worry about.

A strong air suction had started in front of the portal. It was as if a huge fan had been turned on in the other land, and set backward before the doorway. Adam had to hold on to the edge tightly to keep from being sucked in. Behind him, the lava pools hissed. The force of the suction was disturbing the sleeping fires. Adam realized he was on the verge of starting a minor eruption. And he knew he had only to say the word and the doorway would close and everything would return to normal. But for some reason—perhaps it was because he was hanging on for dear life—he couldn't remember what the Reeksvar word for *close* was.

"*Bela!*" he shouted into the howling wind. "Rela! Stela! Mela! Kela! Tela!"

No, none of those were right. Adam feared he was never going to get it. Raising his right leg, he pressed his foot against the side of the doorway and pushed back as hard as he could. He landed on his butt, but was immediately shaken by the suction force. He didn't give it a chance to pull on him again. Reaching out, he grasped the edge of a large black boulder and pulled himself farther away from the howling wind. He did the same with a series of rocks. The lava pools were furious now. Steam gushed toward the ceiling, just about wiping out all visibility. Adam felt the ground shake as he labored to climb to his feet. Something was on the verge of blowing.

Adam made it back to where his friends were waiting.

"What happened?" Sally demanded.

"The Hyeet escaped back to his home," Adam said.

"We saw that," Cindy said. "But why didn't you close the door?"

"Did you shout out the word?" Watch asked.

Adam glanced at the collapsing chamber. "What was the word again?" he asked rather sheepishly.

"*Nela!*" all three of them said at once.

Adam grimaced. "I was close. I should have kept trying."

"Well, you can't try now," Sally said, pointing to what was happening only a few feet from where they stood. There was so much steam, dust, and exploding lava, the magical doorway was completely invisible. Sally shouted over the noise, "We have to get out of here!"

They ran back in the direction of the cold river. It didn't take many turns of the cave to bring them out of the range of the eruption. Soon it was dark again, silent and gloomy. They had saved the Hyeet, but they still didn't know how to save themselves. Worst of all, their meager torches were ready to go out, and they had left their few remaining boards back in the volcanic chamber. They stumbled in the seemingly endless night beside the icy water. Adam had reached the point where he was willing to try anything.

"What if we swim underground?" he asked Watch. "Back the way you came? We might be able to reach the spot where the well comes down. Bum might still be there and be able to help us out."

Watch shook his head. "That's impossible. None of us would be able to swim against the current. I almost drowned, and I was flowing with it. Also, we would never get up the well. It's too hard."

"It's a chance," Cindy said.

"Believe me, it's no chance at all," Watch said. "We have to find another way out."

Sally pointed anxiously at their two waning torches. "We only have a few minutes left. There's no other way out."

But just then Adam had an incredible idea.

It was the best idea he'd had all night.

"Watch," he said. "When you came down the well, could you tell which direction the river beneath you was flowing?"

Watch didn't hesitate. "It was headed toward the ocean. I thought of that. But we all already know there's no cave opening down by the beach."

"And the water is full of sharks," Sally said.

"None of that matters," Adam said. "I have a plan. We're going to keep following this river."

"What if our lights fail?" Sally demanded. "What if we run into a dead end?"

Adam repeated himself, but with an odd confidence in his voice. "None of that matters."

The river rushed forward. They chased it, running now. But they could not run far because the inevitable finally caught up with them. The remaining lumps of lava wrapped around their boards gasped and died. The faint red glow went out. It had been a miserable light, but any light was welcome when darkness was all around. They missed it dearly. They dropped the torches in the black river, but couldn't see as the current carried them away. Their mad dash was finished. They would have to move slowly now, led only by the sound of the water, the touch of their fingers. Adam told them not to lose hope. Someone clasped his hand. He assumed it was Cindy, but it was Sally.

"Did you know I sleep with a night-light on?" she said softly.

"You?" he asked in the perfect dark. "I don't believe it."

Her fingers squeezed his tight. "I've always been afraid of the dark."

"I'm afraid of it now," Cindy whispered from somewhere close.

"I know what I'm doing," Adam said, hoping that he did.

The others had their doubts thirty minutes later.

They ran into a dead end.

The cave just stopped at a stone wall.

The river disappeared under the ground.

End of the road. Nowhere left to go.

Adam heard the sounds of his friends despair all around him. He spoke in what he hoped was an upbeat voice. "Watch," he said. "What time is it?"

Adam knew all of Watch's watches had phosphorescent hands.

"Six-ten in the morning," Watch said. "Why?"

Adam sat down on the ground beside the river, telling the others to do the same. "We're going to wait," he said.

"For what?" Sally asked. "To die?"

"No," he said. "To be rescued."

"No one will come to rescue us," Cindy said sadly.

"I didn't say it would be a person," Adam replied. "Be patient. You'll see."

Several minutes went by while they listened to their breathing. Perhaps they also listened to their own heartbeats.

"I'm getting cold," Sally said finally.

"You'll be warm soon," Adam promised. "A few more minutes."

More minutes crawled by.

Sally started to speak again. But her voice caught in her throat.

Something magical was happening. The water beside them began to glow. It grew in brightness quickly. Soon they were able to see each other again. Adam had to laugh at their astounded faces.

"Is it another magic portal?" Cindy asked.

Adam laughed. "No, it's not magic. Watch, what time is it now?"

Watch checked his timepieces. "Six thirty-six."

Sally gasped. "That's when the sun comes up! We're seeing the light of dawn!"

Adam stood. "Yes. That's it. This stream runs into the

ocean. For us to see the sunlight at all, we must be close to the outside. I bet we only have to swim the length of a backyard pool underwater and we'll be out in the fresh air."

"But how can you know for sure the ocean is right out there?" Cindy asked.

"Taste the water," Adam said.

All three of his friends tried it. "It tastes slightly salty," Cindy said.

"Naturally," Adam said. "Here where the river and the ocean meet, some of the saltwater must push upstream."

"But you got the idea to come here a mile back," Sally insisted. "How could you be sure we'd find the sun?"

Adam laughed again. "I was hoping we'd find it. But all rivers run to the sea, as the old saying goes. Why should this one be different?" He tore off his filthy shirt and kicked off his dirty shoes. "I'm going first. If I'm not back in a minute or two, I don't know what to tell you guys. I've probably gone for milk and doughnuts."

Adam dived in before they could respond.

He was back a minute later, grinning from ear to ear.

"This river comes out right near the jetty," he said. "We're not far from the burned-down lighthouse."

"Oh, no." Cindy groaned. "I hope the ghost is still gone."

"The ghost?" Sally asked. "Who cares about a ghost?"

She stood and began to walk back into the cave. "I'm still worried about that shark we saw last week. There's no way I'm going out this way. I'm hiking back to the reservoir. I don't care if it takes me till next week."

They tried to convince Sally it was a lousy idea, but she was stubborn and wouldn't listen. In the end they had to drag her, kicking and screaming, underwater, and then out onto the jetty. But once she was standing in the fresh air, she quickly forgave them. It looked like it was going to be another sunny day. Sally smiled brightly.

"Who wants ice cream?" she asked. "You can have any flavor you want."

Adam smiled. "As long as it's vanilla?"

Sally pinched his cheek. "That's true. But today, Adam, I feel like treating."

TURN THE PAGE FOR A SNEAK PEAK AT
SPOOKVILLE #4: ALIENS IN THE SKY

ADAM, WATCH, AND SALLY ARE TAKING A RIDE IN
SPACE . . . BUT CAN THEY GET HOME?

1

SPOOKSVILLE SELDOM GOT REALLY HOT.
Nestled among the hills beside the ocean, Spooksville was usually cooled by a breeze preventing it from
becoming uncomfortable, even in the middle of summer. But in the last half of July, only a couple of weeks
after Adam Freeman and his friends got trapped in the
Haunted Cave, the temperature rose sharply. At midday
the thermometer burst past a hundred degrees. To get
away from the heat, Sally Wilcox suggested they head
up to the reservoir.

"We won't go in the water," she said. "You don't want
to do that. But it's always cooler up there."

The four of them: Sally, Adam, Watch, and Cindy

were seated on Cindy Makey's porch, drinking sodas and wiping their sweat-soaked foreheads. Adam stared at the half-burnt-down lighthouse—less than a quarter of a mile away—where he had wrestled with a ghost earlier in the summer. He felt as if he were about to catch fire. He couldn't remember it ever being so hot where he used to live in Kansas City, which was known for its hot summers. He wondered what had brought the heat.

"Why can't we go in the water?" Cindy asked.

"Because you'll die," Sally said simply.

"There are no fish in the reservoir," Watch added. "So there's got to be something unhealthy about the water."

"But Spooksville gets its water from the reservoir," Adam said.

"That's why so many children in this town are born mutated," Sally said.

Cindy smiled. "You were born here, Sally. That explains a lot."

"Not all mutations are bad," Sally replied.

"The water is filtered before we drink it," Watch said.

"What's filtered out?" Adam asked.

"I don't know," Watch said. "But it must be toxic stuff. The filtration plant has a habit of blowing up every couple of years."

"Why's it cooler at the reservoir?" Adam asked.

Sally spoke. "Because Madeline Templeton—the witch who founded this city two hundred years ago—tortured fifty innocent people to death up there. The horror of that event psychically reverberates to this day, making the whole area cold as ice."

Cindy made a face. "And you want to go up there to cool off?"

Sally shrugged. "There is horror on almost every street in Spooksville, if you look deeply enough into the past. On this exact spot, where your house was built, Madeline Templeton once cut off a kid's head and fastened it onto a goat."

"Yuck!" Cindy said. "That's gross."

"Yeah, but the kid was supposed to look like a goat anyway," Watch said.

"Yeah," Sally agreed. "Maybe the witch did him a favor."

"I don't know if she tortured the people at the reservoir to death," Watch continued. "I heard she just made them go swimming in the water, and their skin turned gray and their hair fell out."

"I would rather die than lose my beautiful hair," Sally said, brushing her brunette locks aside.

"I think the area is cooler because of all the subterranean streams," Watch said, finally answering Adam's question. "If you put your ear to the ground, you definitely hear gurgling water."

Adam wiped away more sweat. "Well, should we go up there?"

Cindy was doubtful. "The Haunted Cave is up there."

"The Haunted Cave can't hurt you unless you're stupid enough to go inside it," Sally said.

"Thank you, Sally, for reminding me of my past mistake," Cindy said.

Sally spoke sweetly. "Don't mention it, Cindy."

"The Haunted Cave is high above the reservoir," Watch said. "We can't ride our bikes up that far, but we can take them as far as the reservoir. We could be there in less than twenty minutes." He tugged at his T-shirt, trying to cool off. "I wouldn't mind hanging out up there till it gets dark."

"What do you think is causing this heat?" Adam asked.

"Could be an inversion layer," Watch said.

"Or a curse from Ann Templeton," Sally said. "Madeline Templeton's seductive and evil descendant. She likes the heat. She likes all us kids to suffer in it."

Adam shrugged. "I'm for going," he said, glancing at Cindy, "if it's all right with you."

Sally leaned over and spoke in a *loud* whisper in

Watch's ear. "Notice how our dear Adam doesn't make a move without checking with his sweet Cindy."

Cindy glared at Sally. "He's just being polite. That's spelled P . . . O . . . L . . . I . . . T . . . E. Look it up in the dictionary and check the meaning. I know you've never heard of the word." Cindy spoke to Adam. "My mother doesn't care what I do, as long as I'm home before dark."

"My mother doesn't care what I do as long as I don't die," Sally muttered.

Adam stood. "Then it's decided. We'll ride up and stay until sunset."

The others also stood. Sally, as usual, wanted to have the last word.

"Let's leave before sunset," she said. "You never know what the dark might bring."

2

THE BICYCLE RIDE UP TO THE RESERVOIR
was harder than Adam had imagined. Even though they
had to pedal on an incline most of the way, it was the
temperature that really sapped Adam's strength. He was
feeling wobbly when they arrived and climbed off their
bikes. Fortunately, they had each brought a large plastic
bottle of water.

"I feel a lot cooler, now," Adam said sarcastically as
he opened his bottle and held it up to his lips. "Now that
we're here."

"It's like being in an air-conditioned mall," Cindy
agreed, playing along and reaching for her water bottle.
Her face was red from the sun and exertion.

"Give it a chance. It actually is cooler here," Watch said, stepping to the edge of the reservoir, which was a rough oval, maybe a quarter of a mile long and half that in width. The water was a strange gray color. The surrounding bank was almost entirely devoid of trees. All of their words seemed to die in the air the instant they left their mouths. Watch continued, "It's got to be at least ten degrees cooler."

"I feel refreshed from our ride," Sally said, although she had already plopped down on a boulder and drained half her water bottle. "I think my suggestion was a good one."

Cindy had brought a bag of sandwiches. Finding shade beneath one of the few trees, they sat down and ate. As they munched and talked and drank, Adam did begin to feel cooler. They had set off for the reservoir after four. It was now quarter to five and the heat was just beginning to ease up. But it was still too hot to do much exploring, not that any of them were in the mood to poke around another cave.

Watch had a pack of cards on him and wanted to play poker. Apparently Watch and Sally played together often. Adam was curious, although he had never played the game before and didn't know the rules. But Cindy was uneasy.

"My mother doesn't approve of gambling," Cindy said. "She says it's immoral and disgusting."

"Those two words fit me nicely," Sally said jokingly. "Listen, we're just going to gamble with pebbles. We start with twenty each. It's not really gambling unless you have real money at stake. I mean, how can your mother be upset if you lose a pile of rocks?"

Cindy chuckled. "You have a point. All right, I'll play as long as I don't have to wager my next week's allowance."

Watch explained the rules of five-card stud, and for the next hour or so they played many hands. But Watch and Sally were way ahead of Adam and Cindy when it came to the subtleties of the game. Adam and Cindy quickly lost all their pebbles, and even fierce Sally was steadily withering to Watch's apparent skill. She got down to five pebbles, but finally seemed to be holding a strong hand because she bet two of them at once. Watch was unmoved; he matched her bet.

"I think you're bluffing," he said confidently.

Sally caught his eye. "You think so, babe?" She picked up the remainder of her pebbles. "I raise you another three. Count them."

Watch was unimpressed. "I still think you're bluffing."

Sally sneered. "Thoughts aren't rocks. Put your pebbles where your mouth is."

Watch coolly matched her bet.

Sally was momentarily taken aback.

"What have you got?" Watch asked.

Sally threw her cards down. "Trash. You win. Darn."

"It was an impressive bluff," Adam told Sally.

"I fell for it," Cindy agreed.

"It's not impressive unless it works," Sally muttered.

The sun was near the horizon and they were thinking of returning home when a minor disaster struck. Cindy, still curious about the Haunted Cave, had hiked up to peek at the opening to see if it was closed. They allowed her to go by herself because she had promised not to step inside if it was open. She was on her way back down the hill when she must have stepped on some loose gravel. The ground seemed to go out from under her before she started toppling.

"Cindy!" Adam shouted when he saw what was happening. Sally and Watch looked over, and soon all three were running to Cindy. She hadn't toppled far, maybe twenty feet. But it was enough to pick up several scrapes and bruises. She was wearing shorts, and her legs were bleeding slightly in a few places. But that was not the major problem. As they reached her side, they saw her clutching her right ankle. Adam knelt by her side.

"Did you twist it?" he asked.

Cindy grimaced. "Yeah. It hurts."

"You didn't break it, did you?" Sally asked, concerned. "Your bone isn't sticking out, is it?"

"If you did break it, there won't be an ambulance coming for you," Watch said matter-of-factly. "Spooksville's ambulance drivers have all disappeared."

"Would you two shut up?" Adam said. "Can't you see she's in pain?"

Cindy forced a smile. "It's not too bad. I want to try putting some weight on it."

"You might want to ice it first," Watch suggested.

"Like we just happen to have bags of ice with us," Sally said sarcastically.

Adam helped Cindy up. The moment Cindy put her right foot down, she let out a soft cry. "Ah," she said, breathing heavily. "It really hurts."

Adam pointed to the reservoir. "Maybe you should soak it in the water. It will help with the swelling."

"I wouldn't put my foot in that water if I'd just had sulfuric acid splashed on my toes," Sally said.

Watch strolled over to the water and crouched down. Before any of them could say a word, he reached over and cupped a handful of water. He raised it to his lips and swallowed, then nodded, satisfied.

"It could use a little fluoride, but otherwise it tastes fine," he said.

"We should wait a minute to see if he falls over dead," Sally whispered to Adam and Cindy.

Watch walked back to them. "I don't think it will melt your skin off, Cindy. But leave your shoe on when you put your foot in the water. The pressure of the sides of the shoe will help keep the swelling down as much as the cold water."

"Okay," Cindy muttered as Watch and Adam helped her to a spot close to the water. Cindy sat down and added, "I feel like such a klutz, falling like that."

"I fell," Sally said proudly. "Once. But I regained my balance before causing myself any harm."

"Was the Haunted Cave open or closed?" Watch asked.

"It's still closed," Cindy replied, as she carefully placed her aching ankle into the water. "I didn't have the nerve to try to open it with one of the magic words we learned from the witch." She twitched. "Hey, this water is really cold."

"Some people say the reservoir is bottomless," Sally said. "None of the bodies dumped in here over the years has ever floated back to the surface."

"I think I'm going to talk my parents into buying a

water purifier when I get home," Adam said. He clasped Cindy's hand and spoke in a gentle voice. "Is the pain letting up?"

"Oh, Watch," Sally said, touching her heart. "Look at his bedside manner. He's a born doctor. Dr. Adam— maybe he could be a brain surgeon."

"It feels better, thank you," Cindy said, ignoring Sally. "If I can just soak it for a few more minutes, I may be able to ride back home."

"You can ride a bike with one foot," Sally said. "Jaws does it all the time."

"He's David Green, the kid who lost a leg to the great white shark who stays off our coast," Watch explained in case Adam or Cindy had forgotten.

"You're lucky there are no sharks in the reservoir," Sally added.

"We'll wait here until you feel ready to travel," Adam told Cindy.

Watch nodded toward the west. "The sun is setting. It'll be dark soon."

"This is what I was afraid would happen," Sally said. She took a step away from the water and sat back down. "There's no moon tonight. It will get black as ink up here."

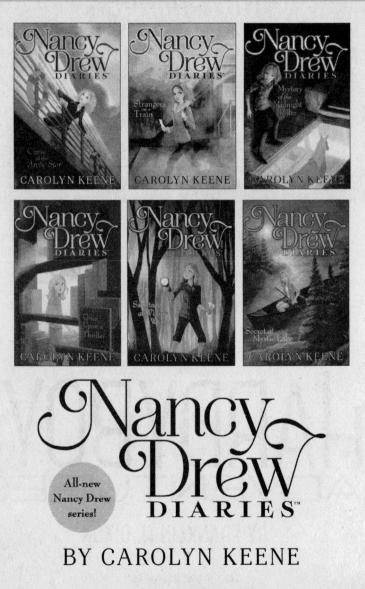